Just Old Ernie

by
Marian R. Bartch
and
Jerry J. Mallett

VANDALIA ROAD • JACKSONVILLE, IL 62650

Published by PERMA-BOUND, Vandalia Road
Jacksonville, Illinois 62650
ISBN: 0-8000-5352-4
Printed in the United States of America

To Tim Erving and Mark Marshall
two exceptional people who share the capacity
to enjoy the humor and delights of life.

CHAPTER ONE

"Ernie," hollered Mom from downstairs, "telephone for you. It's Louise."

"Thanks," I called back. "I'll take it up here." I closed my closet door and hurried to the phone in our upstairs hallway. Louise, who is absolutely the very best friend I have ever had, was calling to check on what I'd be wearing tomorrow — our first day ever at junior high school.

"Hi, Louise . . . oh, yeah, I'm excited too . . . just think, we're really going to be starting a whole new life . . . not yet . . . what are you going to wear? Oh that's neat . . . I'm just not sure . . . hum, I thought about that one too, but I can't decide between that or my . . ."

A noise that sounded suspiciously like the purring of a cat filled the phone. It was followed immediately by a noise that sounded suspiciously like my pest of a little sister trying to shush her crazy cat.

"Shh . . . Claudie . . . shh."

I could just picture Bitsey clutching the phone in one hand and Claudie in the other.

"Bitsey," I said, using my older sister tone of voice, "I know you're listening in on the downstairs phone."

Another loud whisper, "Am not!" was followed by purring that was somewhat muffled.

"Bitsey . . . hang up the phone . . . now!"

I held the receiver away from my ear, knowing what was coming, hoping Louise did too.

BANG!!!

I began, "One of these days . . ." but was cut off by Louise's laughter.

"But Ernie, she's so cute. You're so lucky to have a little sister like Bitsey."

Evidently she had forgotten all about those times that Bitsey had embarrassed us at the lake last summer, but I hadn't. Cute is not how I'd describe Bitsey. Louise might change her mind if she had to put up with her day after day as I do.

I began again, "Anyway, Louise, I hope we're in the same classes . . . but oh, Louise . . . if *he* is, I'll just die! You know what a colossal nerd that big mouth Murphy is. Being on the same bus with him and his half-wit friend is bad enough."

Murphy was the bane of my existence, the fly in the ointment, the blot on the landscape. Everytime . . . and I mean everytime . . . something embarrassing happened to me (through absolutely no fault of my own) he was there to hoot and holler over it.

Before Louise could answer Dad yelled, "Ernie! It's time to eat!"

"Coming, Dad. I have to eat, Louise . . . okay . . . I'll see you on the bus tomorrow. Yeah . . . it is. Okay, first thing in the morning. Bye."

Another command from the cook, "Ernie . . . get off that phone. Dinner's ready."

I hurried downstairs to the dining room. When Dad says it's time for dinner, he really means it. Ever since Mom and Dad switched jobs a year ago and he took over the household chores, dinner is *always* served promptly at six o'clock. This was one of the things he and Mom were always arguing about before the big job change. If you don't know what happened to the Tubb family last year when my life was turned upside-down, you must be the only one in the entire U.S. of A. who doesn't. You see, not only did my dad take over the household duties, but, are you ready, my mom actually began running my dad's hardware business. What's worse is that they've been happy about what each is doing ever since. I, Ernestine Cecilia Tubb, have had to reconcile myself to the fact that I will have to endure this arrangement for the rest of my entire life. Well, to be honest, I have to admit that I don't mind it so much anymore. In fact, Dad does a much better job around the house than Mom ever did, and Mom did so well with the business that we took our first vacation in years last summer. But boy, do I ever have to put up with a lot of teasing from the kids at school . . . especially the mouth Murphy. I bet I could write a book about last summer's vacation and all the problems he and Bitsey caused me to have. That's all behind me now though. Tomorrow I'll officially be a student at the Cecil T. Squat Junior High School.

"We're waiting for you Ernie," yelled Dad impatiently. I slipped into the dining room as quickly as I could.

"Bitsey gotta hotdoggie!" said my irritating three-year-old sister.

"Bitsey," I said. "You had a hotdog last night, and the night before, and the night before. Bitsey, you *always* have a hotdog."

"Bitsey loves hotdoggies," she favored me with a big smile, glowing in what she interpreted as a compliment.

"I know honey," said Mom, "but don't you want to try the delicious ham and cheese casserole Daddy made?"

"NO! Bitsey's hotdoggie more leechious!" declared the sweet little gourmet.

Honestly, I don't know why my parents don't do something with that child!

"What did Louise have to say?" Mom asked.

"Oh, just talking about tomorrow. You know . . . what to wear and all that sort of thing."

"Well," Dad began. I could tell by the tone of his voice that he was starting one of his speeches about LIFE.

"Well," he repeated, clearing his throat "tomorrow you are going to begin a new chapter in your life."

"I certainly hope so," I thought. I was really tired of the same old story . . . it was time for things to get better.

He droned on, "Yes, tomorrow will see you embarking on the first step of your journey through secondary education. Your life's goals are beginning to take shape. You . . ."

The little pipsqueak piped up. "Why is Ernie going to bark?"

We just ignored her . . . that is, we tried to ignore her. Bitsey never tolerates being ignored.

The speechmaker resumed, "You are now . . ."

He was interrupted again.

4

"I wanna hear Ernie bark," the familiar high-pitched whine was creeping into the little darling's voice. "You said she was gonna bark and I . . ."

I couldn't stand it any longer.

"Good grief, Bitsey," I exploded. "Embarking . . . embarking . . . not barking."

"Huh?"

I mustered all of the patience a junior-high girl would be expected to have and explained, "You see, *dear*, embarking means to begin . . . to start a new venture."

She bestowed another of her bright smiles on me, nodded her head in understanding, then asked, "But, Ernie, why do you wanna begin to start barking?"

"Bitsey," Mom said, "eat your nice hotdoggie before it gets cold." She was good at distracting the little genius . . . not that it took much.

Dad attempted to continue his lecture, "Yes, tomorrow, Ernie, you will . . ."

This time it was Mom who interrupted him. "Pete, don't you think this can wait until after we've eaten. Your nice dinner's getting cold."

Dad looked taken back a bit and paused before he said, "But I just want Ernie to realize the importance of these next few years."

I was beginning to wonder if we would ever get to eat.

"Want some of that cat's soup," Bitsey demanded.

"Bitsey," I said, relieved for the change of topic, "it is called *catsup* . . . not cat's soup. Here, here is the bottle of *catsup*."

She took the bottle I offered her saying, "Sank you, Ernie,

sank you for the cat's soup."

How can Louise think she's "cute"?

Unfortunately Mom went right back to the topic of speech, "Honestly, Pete, you'll have Ernie thinking that the success of the rest of her life depends on what happens tomorrow."

Dad was starting to bristle, "Nothing of the sort, Helen. You know that's not what I mean. It's just that certain parts of her life will begin to change and I want her to see how important the coming years are going to be."

"I'm sure she knows that already," Mom said.

Have you ever had the feeling that you are invisible? Well, that's exactly how I was feeling then. I wanted to say, "Look . . . I'm right here. Ernestine Cecelia Tubb. Why not ask me?" But I knew better than to break in on one of their "discussions", which is how my parents refer to their minor arguments.

Dinner ended in a stand-off between Mom and Dad. I remained invisible but my sweet little sister was *very* visible. She managed to interject the reminder — during pauses in the "discussion," and between mouthfuls of "hotdoggie" smothered in the "cat's soup," that her "burpday" was not too far off. As you may guess, "burpday" is Bitsey's garbled way of saying "birthday." Actually the darling's bur . . . birthday . . . is a full three weeks from now but, from the way she's acting, anyone would think it was tomorrow.

The rest of the evening went by very quickly since I had to be totally absorbed in planning my Cecil T. Squat wardrobe. Bitsey did her best to distract me though as she rendered . . . and I do mean rendered . . . her version of the birthday song:

"Happy burpday to me,

Happy burpday to me,
I want three dollies,
Happy burpday to me."

When she first started her rendition . . . four long weeks
ago . . . she only wanted one dolly. Just imagine how many
it will be by birthday time! Before she drifted off to sleep, it
was up to four dollies. Believe it or not, I woke up to *five* dollies!
Luckily for us, she can only count to ten, otherwise, the number
would be in the hundreds on her actual birthday!

"Good morning," chorused Mom and Dad as I entered the
kitchen. I was glad to know I wasn't invisible anymore.

"Morning," I returned.

Dad, actually beaming at me, said, "Pancakes, eggs and
bacon. The best way to get you started on your first day at
junior high."

I was afraid he was going to resume his motivational talk
of the night before, but Mom cut him off by saying, "Oh Ernie, I'm so glad you decided to wear that outfit. You look so
nice in it."

"Thanks, Mom."

"Yes, honey . . . you really do look great," Dad added.

Bitsey wandered into the room, clutching a resigned-looking
Claudie in her arms. She marched right up to Dad and,
thrusting Claudie up toward his face, said, "Claudie says I
should get *six* dollies for my burpday!"

It was a toss-up between who was the most affronted by her
action — Dad or Claudie. Mom intervened by telling our little animal lover that Claudie's friends were waiting for him
in the back yard. She went off, squealing, "Oh, Claudie, let's

7

go see!"

I had no sooner sat down at the table than a long honk sounded in front of our house.

"Oh no . . ." I said, jumping up. "It can't be the bus! It's fifteen minutes early!"

"Here," hollered Dad as I ran out of the kitchen. "Take this!" He shoved two pieces of freshly buttered toast in my hand. I grabbed my purse and notebook with the other.

"Goodbye," I yelled running out the front door.

"Goodluck," Mom called.

"Knock 'em dead!" added Dad.

"Happy burpday," sang you-know-who as she rounded the corner of the house.

As I rushed down the front walk to the waiting bus I felt my notebook slipping. Now, let me tell you, if I had it to do over again, I would let the dumb thing fall and rot right there on our front lawn. But no . . . Ernestine Cecilia Tubb, thinking only of retrieving the notebook, shoved the two pieces of buttered toast into her mouth . . . I'll repeat that . . . into her mouth . . . in order to free that hand. I was quick, but not quick enough. By then the notebook had slipped from my grasp, hit the edge of the walk, and lay there . . . open. Not only open, but sprung, so that the papers were gaily scattering in the breeze. I scurried around, gathering sheets in haphazard fashion. Then, with the notebook under one arm, purse under the other, two handfuls of paper, and butter streaming down her chin from the two pieces of toast stuffed in her mouth, Ernestine Cecilia Tubb made her grand entrance onto bus twenty-nine!

"Oh my," I thought, "what a smashing way to begin my first day at Cecil T. Squat Junior High. Well, at least the day's disaster is over with. Things have to get better from now on."

I clearly remember thinking that to myself. If I had had any inkling of all that would happen to me that first year of junior high, I would have turned around and gone back to bed instead of going up those school bus steps.

CHAPTER TWO

I hurried past Mrs. Angel, our bus driver . . . boy, if ever a person was misnamed she was . . . and collapsed into the seat next to Louise.

"Oh Ernie . . . oh my! Here, let me help you." Louise took the papers and rearranged them in my notebook. I tried to thank her but it's hard to say something . . . anything . . . with two pieces of buttered toast blocking the words. Finally, after swallowing the last bite and wiping the butter off my chin, I was able to ask, "Louise, do you think that this is an omen of what's to come during my next three years at Squat Junior High?" Dad's speech of the night before was beginning to haunt me.

Louise gave me a comforting smile, "Oh, Ernie, of course not. Don't be silly."

"I'm just thankful, Louise, that we're some of the first kids on the bus. What if old Megaphone-Mouth Murphy had gotten on already? Just imagine what he would be saying now!"

"You're sure right about that Ernie. Uh oh, don't look now . . . but here he comes."

10

The bus had made several stops while I was chewing and swallowing and we had finally come to his.

"Hey . . . hey . . . if it isn't the Bobbsey twins!" Of course he had to yell this at the top . . . and I mean the very top . . . of his voice as he walked down the aisle. And if you are wondering where he chose to sit, let me tell you. Naturally . . . where else . . . he slid into the seat behind ours.

"Hey, I hear that the courses are really tough at Squat. Did you hear that? Ernie? Louise?"

You know, John can actually resemble a real human being when he isn't trying to impress one of his stupid friends. But since Louise and I had fallen into his "I'm really a nice guy" trap before we just gave one another the eye and ignored his question.

"Do you know where we're supposed to go first?" I asked.

"No," Louise answered. "I hope someone is there to help us find our way."

Murphy, determined to be a part of our conversation, said, "Norm told me that the ninth-grade student council members will be stationed around the halls to tell us where to go."

"And who is Norm?" I asked, forgetting to ignore him.

"He's a ninth-grader whose parents play bridge in the same club as my parents."

Just then the bus stopped and one of the Mouth's friends, Albert, got on.

"Hey . . . Murph!" he called as he fell into the seat beside John. "Phew . . . I sure smell something awful! And it's real close. Don't you smell something, Murph?"

That was the end of Mr. Nice Guy.

"Now that you mention it, Al, I sure do."

Louise and I exchanged glances which said to pretend we didn't hear the drips.

"Did you talk to Ellie last night?" I asked her.

"Ugh . . . the smell is really getting to me," said the Mouth loudly.

"Yes . . . I did talk to Ellie, Ernie." Louise was making it clear that we were not interested in the conversation of the two stupids sitting behind us. Now that was probably a mistake on our part since they simply kept getting louder with each subsequent comment. Louise and I continued our chatter charade anyway.

"Ellie said she would meet us in front of the school," Louise continued.

"Oh, Murph . . . that smell! I can't breathe . . . I'm going to PASS OUT!"

"That's good Louise. That way the three of us can go in together, just as we've always done."

"UGH . . . UGH . . . UGH . . . GASP! This is it, Murph. I can't last any longer!"

"What's Ellie wearing?"

"I'll help you Al. I'll pinch your nose. There now, breathe through your mouth."

"I'll try," was the nasal response.

"She didn't know when I talked to her, Ernie."

Albert, in a nasal voice, rising in pitch, declared, "I can't stand it any longer!"

His declaration was followed by a blood-curdling scream as the idiot staggered out of his seat . . . clutching his throat

. . . and fell to the floor of the bus.

His startling act had an electrifying effect on all of the occupants of the bus. Conversations ceased as everyone's eyes focused on the now still figure of the star performer of bus twenty-nine.

Before anyone could say anything, the bus veered sharply to the right. Albert's gasp-of-death must have had a chilling effect on Mrs. Angel. Yells and screams came from various parts of the bus as, after several bone-shattering jolts, it stopped, listing badly to one side.

There was dead silence for about one second, then more yells and screams. Louise and I, untangling ourselves from each other and the metal seat legs, tried to get up from the floor where we had been thrown.

The deep, husky voice of Mrs. Angel boomed through all of the chaotic noise of the passengers, "Stop that racket! At once . . . do you hear? No one is hurt . . . so shut . . . stop it!"

I was wondering how she could possibly know that when she went on. "Okay . . . now, you turkeys . . . which one of you is responsible for this disaster?"

I wanted to tell her that SHE was the one driving the bus, but then thought better of opening my mouth.

She continued bellowing as she struggled down the slanting aisle to where John and Albert lay at the bottom of a tangle of kids all heaped together. As the others scrambled up John and Albert were left to face her towering wrath.

"Your names . . . I wanna know your names . . . now!"

"J-J-John Murphy."

"Ah, Albert Finwit."

13

"Alright, you nerds . . . you don't have to admit to being the troublemakers, but if you don't I'll break your legs!"

Albert was apparently quite shaken, in more ways than one as he said, "Honestly, I really never meant to cause all this."

"You two-bit turnips," blared our guardian angel, her lip curling. I ought to . . ." then catching herself, she commanded, "Okay, all you kids. Pick yourselves up and follow me out of the bus . . . and make it snappy!"

A bruised and disheveled band slowly made its way up the slanting aisle to the gaping door. As I stepped out of the bus I saw that the front wheel had come to rest in the ditch that ran along the roadside. The way my morning had been going I would not have been a bit surprised if a flash flood had swept me away as I crossed the ditch.

"Alright, you kids . . . stay over there . . . and I mean STAY!"

Mrs. Angel was pointing to the other side of the ditch. I noticed that she gave John and Albert the full benefit of a malevolent glare that made me shiver. It obviously had its intended effect upon the bus wreckers for they both slunk behind the rest of us trying to make themselves invisible. I figured they would become acquainted with the principal of Squat before any of the rest of us knew who he was. I experienced a momentary pang of sympathy for them which was immediately eased by my remembering their smell routine.

As Mrs. Angel made her way up the steps, she called back, "I'm going to try to back this bus out of the ditch . . . I don't want any more nonsense from any one of you while I'm doing it!"

So we stood there, our eyes glued to the sight of our

14

precariously-tilted bus, as Mrs. Angel started the engine. Bus twenty-nine emerged ever-so-slowly from the ditch until it was on an even keel once more. Once that was accomplished its driver leaned out and hollered, "Alright, you guys . . . get back here where you belong . . . NOW!"

We all scurried across the ditch and re-boarded the bus. Let me tell you that the remainder of the bus ride, short as it was, thank goodness, was made in a death-like silence. No one wanted to bring forth the vengeful wrath of the Angel who appeared to be on the verge of a mighty eruption!

CHAPTER THREE

"It is my pleasure to be the first to welcome you formally to the Cecil T. Squat Junior High School," boomed a deep voice. "I am Mr. Dratt, your Vice-Principal. Mr. Sumkins, your Principal, has been detained in his office until an emergency situation concerning a mishap on a school bus is cleared up."

I nudged Louise and she gave me a low groan. We were sitting beside each other on bleachers that had been pulled out from a wall in a room that was both the gymnasium and auditorium. The one good thing about the morning was that Louise and I were in the same homeroom.

"I am glad to see that our new seventh-graders know how to enter the gym for assembly . . . quietly!"

We looked at each other, not sure whether to take his comment as a compliment or a threat. From the scowl on his face, I figured it was meant as a warning.

"Now at Squat we have rules," thundered Mr. Dratt. "And everyone must understand that these rules are to be obeyed!"

I wondered why Mr. Dratt bothered to use the microphone. I was quite sure that I would have been able to hear his loud pronouncements at home . . . in bed with the pillow clamped over my head!

He continued. "Yes . . . obeyed. Obeyed by one and all. Now, rule number one. We *walk* in the hallways. We do *not* run. At *no* time do we run in the hall. Rule number two. When we . . ."

We were spared from hearing the rest of what was probably a long list of rules by the entrance of a man who walked hurriedly up to the stage and positioned himself in front of the microphone.

Mr. Dratt, who had quickly stepped aside, leaned across him to say, "We'll continue this later. But for now, here is your Principal, Mr. Sumkins."

There was a smattering of applause from the teachers as the principal took over, saying, "Thank you, Mr. Dratt for steering the ship for me. I was unfortunately delayed by some rather unpleasant business."

Louise and I looked at each other knowingly.

"But now I want to say that all of us here at Squat Junior High welcome you aboard. I like to think of our school as a ship . . . a ship that will transport each of you safely through the rough and sometimes stormy seas of your voyage to knowledge. Think of your teachers as the ship's mates."

I couldn't help but notice that some of the teachers rolled their eyes at each other on hearing this statement.

In a voice vibrating with enthusiasm Mr. Sumkins continued, "And . . . think of *me* as the *captain* of the ship!"

Someone behind us whispered, "I think I'm getting seasick." The comment generated a few giggles which quickly stopped as Mr. Dratt, a fierce glare on his face, took steps in our direction. The captain of the good ship Squat, totally ignoring this disturbance, continued welcoming his new passengers aboard.

"The captain and all of the mates," he paused here to glance around at the teachers who were by now shifting uneasily in their seats, "are here to help make the waters as smooth as possible. To do anything less would dishonor the memory of the man for whom our school is named ... *Captain* Cecil T. Squat. Yes," as he went on a faraway look appeared in his eyes, "our school is named for that great and brave man who was born and raised and lived out his life in our very own Pleasant Valley."

A low moan escaped from Louise. I knew exactly what she was thinking ... not *that* story again. Every child in Pleasant Valley had heard praise heaped on the memory of Cecil T. Squat before. Over and over again. Our fifth-grade teacher even made each of us build a model of his ferryboat. Yes, you heard right ... I said ferryboat. John Murphy got into trouble because he built his model bottom-end up, sinking into a sea of blue tinted cotton batting. Our teacher denounced it as an insult to the memory of such an outstanding Pleasant Valley hero.

BOOM!! A clap of thunder brought me out of my day dream. I looked out the narrow windows at the top of the gym but the sun was shining brilliantly. BOOM!! When it happened again I realized it was not really thunder but Mr. Sumkins pounding on the podium to make a point.

"Yes," he said loudly, "over twenty thousand crossings and he never (pound) missed (pound) one (pound) of (pound) them (pound)!"

I conjured up a picture of Captain Squat, enmeshed in the cobwebs that covered the ferryboat, hanging on to the wheel, peering glassy-eyed into a dense fog.

"Back and forth . . . back and forth," *our* ship's captain swayed with his words. "Day and night . . . night and day . . . until," his voice broke, but he took a deep breath and recovered enough to drone on, ". . . until that fateful night that saw the sinking of the S.S. Petunia . . . saw her slipping into her watery grave."

Louise, covering her mouth with her hand, whispered, "I don't care if that was his wife's name. It's the dumbest name for a ferryboat I ever heard."

I nodded in an agreement as Mr. Sumkins forged ahead in recalling the harrowing demise of the S.S. Petunia.

"And to think . . . to think, boys and girls . . . what happened was no fault of Captain Squat. No, none whatsoever. Oh, if only the first-mate had been alert . . . the entire tragedy could have been avoided. If only the first-mate had untied the S.S. Petunia *before* Captain Squat threw the engine full-throttle in reverse. If only the first-mate had sounded the alarm at first sight of the splintering wood as the dock was being pulled apart. If only the first-mate had warned Captain Squat about the weakened throttle handle *before* our brave and quick-thinking captain thrust it forward to save the dock *and* the S.S. Petunia. And indeed he would have saved them both if only the throttle handle had not broken off in his hand. If only he hadn't lost valuable seconds holding it up and staring at it. Oh, but boys and girls, remember this and remember it well . . . this

19

proved to be Captain Squat's finest hour. For, as the S.S. Petunia was driven head-on into what was left of the end of the dock, she began to list precariously to her side. Screams could be heard as the passengers panicked at the sight of Petunia's stern slowly sinking into the icy depths of the harbor. It was the cool head of the captain that saved the day. (At least the first-mate had the presence of mind to revive him after he had been knocked unconscious by the force of the collision.) Then, true to the tradition of the sea, Captain Squat proceeded to help all, and I do mean *all*, of the passengers to the safety of the partially submerged dock. And I want it remembered," ordered Mr. Sumkins "that Captain Cecil T. Squat (pound) was the last person (pound) to leave the ship (pound). And, I must add, just seconds before her bow slid off the dock and sank."

The room was deadly silent. Everyone, including all of the teachers, were simply staring at Mr. Sumkins, who appeared to be overcome with this account. He was standing motionless, clutching the podium, gazing off into space. Then, shaking his head slightly, he looked around the gym, cleared his throat and quietly said, "And *that* is why, boys and girls, each and everyone of you should be proud to be a crew member of the Cecil T. Squat Junior High School."

I have to admit that although I had heard the story of the brave captain many times before, I had never heard anyone, and I mean *anyone*, tell it with such force as Mr. Sumkins had.

"And now," added the storyteller, "I'd like to introduce our guidance counselor, Miss Smoothly, to you. She will tell you a little about running our ship and how you can help us to keep it in shape . . . shipshape, that is. Ha, ha. Get it? Shipshape!"

"Good grief," I moaned to myself. I was beginning to understand why some of the older kids referred to him as Mr. Numbkins.

Miss Smoothly took over.

"Thank you, Mr. Sumkins," said Miss Smoothly. "Boys and girls, your homeroom teachers will discuss your academic schedules with you. What I am here for is to inform you of all the opportunities each of you has *beyond* the academic program. Opportunities to become involved in sports, the music program and various clubs. You will be hearing much more about the many activities and I would personally like to see each of you become active in at least one of them."

Louise and I nudged each other. We had already discussed joining a couple of clubs.

Miss Smoothly continued, "In fact, I have two announcements to make right now. All boys interested in playing football need to meet with Coach Dirk in his classroom after school on Wednesday. That is room 209."

Several of the boys sitting near us gave the thumbs-up sign to one another.

"And," smiled Miss Smoothly, "any girl wishing to try out for the junior varsity cheerleading squad needs to meet with Mrs. Volumous after school Thursday . . . in the gym. Right here, girls."

I don't know about Louise, but I didn't hear another word of what was said after that. The next thing I knew, everyone was getting up to leave.

The first thing Louise said as we reached the bottom of the bleachers was, "Oh, Ernie . . . cheerleading . . . oh, Ernie!"

"Oh, Louise," I gushed, "do you think we could? Could we really make the squad?"

"Why not?" She was almost jumping up and down in her excitement. "Remember at the lake last summer?"

"Well yes, Louise . . . but we were only cheering for the boat races."

"Ernie," she said, coming to a dead stop to look at me, "We were really good. Everybody said so."

"Oh, Louise," I poked her to keep on walking, "*everybody* consisted of my mother and father."

"Well, we *were* good and I think we should try out."

"Well, sure . . . so do I, but I'm scared already."

"Me too," sighed Louise. Then added as we turned into our homeroom, "let's practice after school today at my house."

"Okay . . . at least we can try. We have nothing to lose!"

How could I have believed that . . . nothing to lose . . . as I was soon to learn, I should have known better.

CHAPTER FOUR

Rickity rack. Rickity rack.
We've got the game, smack in the sack.
Our team is hot. What we're not,
Are losers . . . no, we're from Squat!

"Oh Louise, I'm so nervous." I had to shout a little to be heard over the cheers.

"Me too." She managed a warm smile. I had to keep swallowing.

The two of us, along with twenty other seventh-grade girls, were sitting on a section of bleachers pulled out from the gym wall. After watching the four girls in cheerleader uniforms for a moment, I nudged Louise and moaned, "They're so good. We don't stand a chance. I just know it. We might as well go home right now."

"Well they should be good, Ernie, they're last year's cheering squad. We'd be just as good if we'd had a year's practice . . . probably better."

I really admire Louise's self-confidence. Of course, it helps not to be involved in one disaster after another as I always am. I did feel encouraged by her words, though.

"I suppose you're right, but I'd give anything . . . well, almost anything . . . to be chosen to be a member of the Squat Squad."

"Oh, me too," Louise answered dreamily.

"Maybe we should have practiced more last night." I was still worried.

"Good grief, Ernie . . . we practiced last night and the night before that and the night before that." Then, with a smile, she added, "You know, your mom and dad would have thrown us out of the house if we had done our cheer one more time."

"I know, I know. It's just that I'm nervous. Actually, being chosen or not chosen could affect our entire junior high careers." I suddenly realized I sounded like my dad.

"Now you're making *me* nervous. Look, Ernie, why don't we . . ."

She was interrupted by Mrs. Volumous, "Alright, girls, each of you has a card with a number on it. That's the order in which you will try out for the Squat Squad."

I looked at my card and said to Louise. "At least I'm not first."

"Thank goodness, I'm not either."

"Now," Mrs. Volumous continued her instructions, "when your number is called go to the center of the gym and lead the cheer you've been given. It's one of the ones that members of last year's squad just demonstrated for you."

As Mrs. Volumous continued to talk, my thoughts drifted back over the past few days at Squat Junior High. It seemed I had been there much longer. Actually, everything had gone very well except for that disastrous start on bus ride twenty-

24

nine. The one thing that really bothered me was that John Murphy and I were partners in science lab. "Yuk!" I thought, envisioning the show-off doing disgusting things and blaming *me*. I was brought back to the present by Louise saying, "Wish me luck."

"Oh, sure, Louise . . . yes . . . good luck. You'll do great."

Louise strode to the center of the gym and waited for Mrs. Volumous to give the signal for her to start her cheer.

A thousand butterflies fluttered in my stomach as Louise began.

"Good grief," I thought, "how will I feel when it's my turn?" I would soon find out.

"Give me an S . . ." Louise yelled and raised a gold pompon with her left hand.

"Give me an Q . . ." she continued, raising the other pompon.

"Give me a U . . ." .

"Gosh," I thought, "Louise is really good. She's sure to make the squad."

We had always practiced together at home so this was the very first time I had ever had a chance to watch her. She was doing a super job. I only hoped I would do half as well.

As soon as she finished she rushed back to the bleachers. "How'd I do?"

"Louise, you were great. Absolutely great!"

"Oh, Ernie . . . do you really mean it?"

"Yes . . . I really do. You did a super cheer. If only I . . ."

"Number eight!" called Mrs. Volumous.

"Oh no . . . that's me!"

25

"Good luck, Ernie," Louise said.

I began my walk to the center of the gym. Well, let me tell you, if I thought I was nervous watching Louise, I was sadly mistaken. Until now, I didn't know what nervous was. Nothing . . . not even that death-defying waterslide ride of last summer . . . could begin to reach what I felt now. I could hardly pick up the pom-pons because my hands were shaking so much. As I straightened back up, my pom-pons dangling from my trembling fingers, I heard a strange buzzing in my ears.

"Good grief," I thought. "I'm about to pass out!"

I took a deep breath and said to myself, "Now look here, Ernestine Cecelia Tubb, you have to get hold of yourself. You are *not* going to pass out in front of everyone here."

"Okay, number eight, let's go," Mrs. Volumous gave a smile of encouragement. "Show us your stuff."

I truly hoped that my "stuff" would not consist of fainting dead away on the gym floor as I began my cheer.

"Give me an S . . ." I shouted, thrusting the pom-pon in my left hand high in the air.

I glanced at Louise and she was all smiles.

"Give me a Q . . ." I whipped the other pom-pon into the air.

"Give me a U . . ." I yelled, bringing both hands down to my hips. I was feeling more confident now for Louise and I had practiced this so many times.

"Gosh," I remember thinking, "this isn't so bad." Oh, brother . . . I should have known better. I *should* have had sense enough to take those stupid pom-pons, handed them to the next girl in line and walked straight out of the gym while I could still hold my head high. But did I do it? No, of course not . . . not me . . . not good old believing-in-everything-turning-out-right-Ernie. Without the slightest inkling of the impending disaster, I shouted, "Give me an A . . ." crouched down to ready myself for the final, and I do mean final, leap up in the air.

"Give me a T . . ." I screamed, leaping high into the air and doing a scissors kick.

Unfortunately as I twisted my wrist to give an added flair to my cheer, I lost my grip on the pom-pon in my left hand. Faster than the speed of light, it was transformed into a lethal projectile hurtling through space. The blood drained from my head as I stood there. I was helpless to stop the movement of the runaway pom-pon. This, of course, was pure undeniable disaster, but then . . . then . . . things got *worse*. For as I stood there, I heard the all-too-familiar voice oozing glee and smugness, drifting from the doorway, "Hey, hey . . . look here. Little Bo-Peep has lost her pom-pon. Baa, baa, baa!"

I moaned to myself, "Oh, isn't this just great. Big-mouth Murphy *would* have to be watching. He'll have a great story to tell on the bus tomorrow. Maybe I can get Dad to bring me so I won't have to stand his gloating."

Well, there wasn't any more time to think of the Mouth because my pom-pon found its landing place as it zeroed in on Mrs. Volumous. Yes, you did hear right. I am telling you that it made the nicest three-point landing you could ever hope to see . . . right on the *top* of Mrs. Volumous' head! Head rhymes with dead and that's what I knew I was as far as the squad was concerned. I had never felt so awful in all of my life.

There was a momentary dead silence, then Mrs. Volumous started to giggle. Then the others joined in. The giggles soon turned into hysterical laughter until there wasn't a dry eye in the house . . . that is, of course, if you did not count yours truly. Poor Ernestine Cecelia Tubb just had to stand there feeling humiliated . . . her mouth open and face a bright pink.

I could hear Murphy and his jerky friends out in the hallway hollering something about Ernie's baa-d death squad.

Finally Mrs. Volumous was able to regain control of herself long enough to say, "You may sit down, number eight."

Then, while attempting to keep a straight face, she added, "Number eight, you . . . you . . . really did . . . did do . . . a very . . . it wasn't really . . . your . . . your . . . fault . . . that . . . that . . ."

Then she completely broke down again. Try as she might, Mrs. Volumous just couldn't say any more.

CHAPTER FIVE

We're from Squat.
Like it or not.
Our team is hot.
Cause we're from Squat!"

"Oh darn," complained Louise. "I keep forgetting to turn on the word 'hot'."

"Let's do it one more time," I suggested.

Louise and I were in my backyard practicing a few of the cheers for the Squat Squad. Yes, in spite of everything, I had made the cheerleading squad. It was an absolute miracle. I figured I was only chosen because Mrs. Volumous felt sorry for me, but I didn't care *why* I was chosen as long as I was on the squad. Naturally Louise made the squad too. After all, she was clearly the best in the try outs.

Gimme a cow.
Gimme a oink.
Gimme a cow.

Gimme a dog.
Gimme a cow.
Gimme a piggy.
Gimme a Claudie.
Gimme . . .

"Oh, for Heaven's sake, Bitsey. Will you please keep quiet! Louise and I have to practice for *real* cheerleading. Besides, your cheer doesn't make a bit of sense."

"Does so!" My sweet little sister punctuated her words by stamping her foot. "Claudie likes doin' cheeries. He does, he does, he does."

Bitsey was holding our long-suffering cat with an iron grip.

"Oh, my, yes . . . I can certainly tell by the way he's squirming to get away that Claudie loves doin' cheeries."

"Oh, Ernie, she's so cute," Louise said.

For the life of me, I do not, never have, and never will understand how Louise could possibly think the little pest is cute. If she had to *live* with her like I do you can bet she'd sing a different tune.

A mournful-sounding, "Moooo . . . moooo . . ." came floating down our driveway.

"Oh, brother, that's all we need," I told Louise, "Chester the cow."

"Chester, Chester," squealed Bitsey. "We doin' cheeries. Cheeries, cheeries. Claudie and me doin' cheeries!"

"Moooo . . . what's doin' cheeries?"

Without any warning whatsoever, Bitsey kicked her foot high in the air and screamed, "Gimme a cow!"

30

Claude looked as if he had just seen the headless-horseman galloping through the backyard. His body went stiff as a board and his eyes bugged out of his head. One of two things was happening . . . he was either being strangled or was scared half-witless . . . or maybe a little of both.

"Moooo . . . I can do that," said Chester and kicked *his* foot in the air.

Fortunately for Claude, our little cheerleading expert became so engrossed in teaching the cow how to do his kick, the right way, that is . . . that she loosened her grip. Claude shot out of her arm faster than a speeding bullet and dashed around the corner of the house. This was one of the few sensible things I had ever seen Claude do. The most sensible thing he could do would be to find another family . . . one without a three-year-old tyrant.

Oh, by the way, if you're wondering about Chester mooing, don't even try to guess why he does. I am sure even the most knowledgeable child psychologist would be baffled by his behavior. It's just that every other week or so he becomes . . . and I do mean becomes . . . a different animal. He not only makes its sound until you think you will go completely out of your mind, he also takes on all of the other characteristics of the animal such as chewing grass or sniffing at trees. My mother says Chester is just going through a phase. Chester is simply a ding-bat. I am sure that's why he and Bitsey get along so well together. I am also sure that Chester's third-grade teacher is absolutely thrilled to have a cow in her classroom.

"Ernie . . . Louise," Dad hollered from the kitchen window, "could you come inside for a minute, please?"

31

"Sure, Dad."

I turned to Louise and said, "Since we've already been interrupted, let's take a break. We need one anyway . . . especially from you-know-who and her companion, the cow."

We raced up the steps and burst through the back door to the strains of "Gimme a pig. Mooo. Gimme a donkey. Mooo. No, Chester, not that way. This way. Chester, watch me. Kick a cheerie like this."

"What do you want, Dad?"

"Oh, Ernie, Louise . . . I sure hope you will be willing help to me."

"Why, of course we will, Mr. Tubb."

"Help you do what?" I asked suspiciously. You notice that I was not as willing to commit myself before finding out just exactly what it was that Dad wanted. I had fallen into this trap once too often.

"It's Bitsey . . ."

"Oh no, Dad . . . oh no!" I cut him off. "Louise and I have to keep on practicing our cheers. We simply *cannot* baby-sit her now."

"Oh, Ernie, sure we can," Louise said.

"Ernie," Dad said, "this has nothing to do with babysitting Bitsey. It's about her birthday next Saturday. I have everything taken care of except the games. It would really be helpful if you two would plan the games."

"Oh, gosh," Louise said. "That sounds like fun. Doesn't that sound like fun, Ernie? We'd love to. Ernie?"

I'll have to admit I was a bit surprised by Dad's request. It did, in fact, sound like fun. Now that just shows you what bad judgment Ernestine Cecelia Tubb has. Fun. I should have answered, "Why thank you, father dear, for thinking of us, but my schedule simply won't permit me to have such fun." Instead I replied, "Well, okay. It sounds easy enough. I guess so, as long as you keep Bitsey from bothering us when we're getting ready." I would live to regret my impulsive decision.

"Oh, that's great. It will really save me a lot of time. I sure do appreciate it, girls."

"How many will there be at the party, Mr. Tubb?"

"We've invited seven of Bitsey's friends . . . so count on eight for each game."

I was astonished to discover that Bitsey *had* seven friends, but caught myself from saying it just in time. Dad can be a bit too sensitive about my honest criticisms of his youngest daughter.

"Ernie, let's go up to your room and decide on the games right now," said Louise enthusiastically. "Gosh, this is going to be so much fun."

"We might as well," I agreed, with a little less enthusiasm. "We certainly can't get in any more *worthwhile* practice until the cow moves along to graze in another pasture."

CHAPTER SIX

Happy burpday today,
Happy burpday today,
Bitsey gets all her dollies,
On her burpday today.

Yes, you guessed it . . . the big day finally arrived. I was as glad as Bitsey since it would mean she'd stop singing her inane songs about her "burpday."

Louise and I were in the backyard with the "burpday" girl and her friends, helping with the games as we had promised to do.

"Come on, Buffy, line up over here with the rest," I said for what seemed like the hundredth time. "Everybody's going to have a lot of fun playing this game. There is a prize for the winner, too." I hoped that the possibility of winning a prize would make her a little more cooperative.

"I wanna go home," whined the little party-goer.

"I'll line up with you, Buffy." Louise took her hand and they walked together to the starting line. "We'll be partners."

"Boy, that Louise," I thought admiringly, "she sure has a way with kids."

I was beginning to feel apprehensive about our decision to help with the games. Just trying to get Bitsey and her seven friends to line up was almost impossible, let alone trying to keep everyone in a happy party mood. Ernestine Cecelia Tubb, never one to give up without a good try, began to explain the game.

"Alright, boys and girls, we're ready to begin. Now, when I say 'go' you will all . . . . NO . . . . NO . . . . STOP . . . . STOP . . . . STOP . . . . I DIDN'T SAY 'GO' YET! GET BACK HERE IN LINE!"

I shot a "Help me!" look at Louise, but she was laughing so hard all she could do was to wave.

I made a superhuman attempt to regain control of the all-too-anxious-game players.

"Good. That's right, Justin. Very good, Andrea. Oh, boys and girls, look at how Justin and Andrea have lined up so nicely. Let's all do the same."

"He's in *my* place," Sammy complained, giving Chester a little push.

"Chester, since you're older than the rest, why don't you move over a little?"

"Okay . . . quack, quack, quack."

I'm sure you don't need three guesses to determine the animal Chester had turned into for this week.

"Lucy," Louise said, "come over here next to Sammy."

With everyone back in place, I resumed my explanation.

"There now. What you are . . ."

"Happy burpday to me,

Happy burpday to . . ."

"Bitsey, dear," I was losing my patience, "please, dear, stop singing and listen!"

"Don't have to . . . it's my burpday."

I had to grit my teeth as I replied, "I know, honey, And that's why Louise and I are trying to help you and your little friends play games and have a good time." My voice rose a bit in pitch as I added, "So *please* . . . dear . . . stop singing and LISTEN!"

Without giving her a chance to answer, I continued, "I'm going to explain the game now, boys and girls. I don't want any of you to begin running until I've finished telling you what you are to do in this race. Now listen carefully.

1. You are to run to the fence.

2. Look for a penny hidden somewhere near the fence.

3. Pick up the penny and bring it back to me.

4. The first one to hand me a penny wins the prize."

It seemed to me that even the most confused of Bitsey's friends could follow my clear directions.

"Quack, quack . . . oh, a surprise prize. Maybe I won't want it."

"Well, if the duck doesn't want to be in this game he doesn't have to play," my temperature was rising.

"Quack, quack. I'll play."

I couldn't help glaring at the ding-bat duck, "Well, we certainly are the honored ones!"

I looked at the line of players and called, "On your mark. Get set!"

"I gotta go puddle," Buffy stepped out of line.

36

"Pardon?" I asked. "What did you say, Buffy?"

"I gotta go puddle . . . now!"

I stared at her blankly and hunched my shoulders. Louise came to the rescue again, "I think she means bathroom."

"Buffy, is that it? Do you have to go to the bathroom?"

"Yes . . . NOW!"

"I'll take her," said Louise, "you go on with the game."

As Louise hurried Buffy into the house so she could make her puddle, I reminded the group, "Now remember that you are to run to the fence, find a penny, and then run back to me. On your mark . . ."

"Quack quack, you already said that."

"Good grief, Chester, I was starting over."

"Quack quack, okay, Ernie."

"Get set . . . . GO!"

Well, what happened next was pure pandemonium. If I had planned for it, it couldn't have gone better. I mean, it is impossible for anyone to imagine the frenzied chaos that followed my "GO!" command. All of the participants were yelling and screaming and Justin was pushing everyone else down and taking the found pennies away.

"Boys and girls!" Even though I was shouting at the top of my voice, there was no way I could be heard over the shrieks, yells, screams, and quacks down at the fence. I rushed over and shouted again, "STOP THAT THIS INSTANT!"

I had their attention for about one second, then "Quack, quack, I found another penny!" started the free-for-all all over again. In the midst of all of this, Chester's dog, Tinkerbell, who had a gigantic body and a midget-sized brain, bounded right over the fence to join in the kill-your-friend-for-a-penny game.

I didn't know what to do. There was no way I could stop the mayhem. Thank goodness, Dad and Mom came racing out of the back door.

"What on earth is going on out here?" Dad roared.

"Bitsey, Chester, Andrea," Mom yelled, as she grabbed two of them. Dad grabbed another two and the pleasant game came to an abrupt end.

Dad glared at me, "Ernie, I thought you were in charge out here."

"We were only playing a game," I began weakly, "I don't know exactly what went wrong."

"Well, I don't think we need any more games like *this* one," Mom gave me the raised eyebrow routine as she spoke. Then, looking at Chester, she said, "Chester, please take Tinkerbell home right now."

"Quack, quack, okay, Mrs. Tubb."

Louise and Buffy came hurrying out the back door as the dog and duck made their way down the driveway. Louise took one look as the disheveled group and gasped, "Oh, Ernie, what happened?"

Buffy started to whine, "I didn't get to play. Everybody got to play but me."

"Yeah, looky . . . I got two pennies," Justin proclaimed.

I was personally surprised his pockets were not bulging with pennies considering the big-time wrestling techniques he had applied in our friendly little game.

"I want a penny," Buffy said, not easily put off.

"Here," said Dad handing her a penny he had pulled from his pocket. "This penny is for being such a good girl."

"Oh, brother," I thought to myself, "she gets a penny for going puddle." I marveled that there weren't seven other puddles right then and there in the backyard.

"We'll have more games later," said Mom. Then, looking directly at me, "Nice quiet games."

"Boy, doesn't that just figure," I thought. "The little demons create havoc and I, poor old Ernie, trying to help out, get the blame."

"But now," Mom continued, "now, we are all going to sing happy birthday to Bitsey while her father brings out the birthday cake."

I hadn't even realized that Dad had gone into the house. A card table, decorated with a birthday party tablecloth, had been set up outside. Balloons and party hats and favors were on the table. Dad put the cake right in the middle, somehow managing to carry it so that the candles remained burning.

Bitsey, of course, led the group of merry party-goers in her favorite song, "Happy burpday to me, Happy burpday . . . ."

A chorus of "Quack, quack, quack to you," alerted us to the return of the duck, minus his dog friend.

Everyone crowded around the table to admire the cake.

"Oh, Mr. Tubb," Louise breathed, "the cake is just beautiful."

The baker beamed at her compliment, "Thank you, Louise."

Mom smiled at the burp . . . birthday . . . girl and told her, "Make a wish now, honey . . . then blow out all of the candles."

Bitsey shrieked, "Bitsey wanna dolly!" then blew out a puff of air. The candles remained lighted.

"Bitsey, you're going to have to blow harder that that," Mom said.

Bitsey took a deep breath and tried again. Nothing. Not even one candle so much as flickered.

That's when yours truly came up with her flash of inspiration . . . what I used to call an "Ernie special." Or so I thought at the time.

"Maybe we should *all* help Bitsey," I suggested. "It may be the *only* way we'll get a taste of the birthday cake."

Well, when I'm wrong I am *really* wrong. That there was indeed another way one could "get a taste of the birthday cake" was beyond the realm of my wildest imagination.

It seems that when Dad, obviously in a hurry, set up the card table he neglected to secure the latch on one of the legs. Now you may be wondering just who was standing right next to the ready-to-collapse-at-the-slightest-touch table leg. Well, wonder no longer. It was, naturally, poor old Ernie, completely unaware of impending disaster.

Mom said, "Oh, what a good idea, Ernie. Alright, boys and girls, let's all put our heads together and help Bitsey blow out the candles. Everybody blow when I count to three."

"One."

Eight little heads leaned over the card table.

"Two."

Eight pairs of lips puckered up for a mass assault on the candles.

"Three."

Eight little bodies surged against the card table.

"Eeeooow!" I screamed as the card table leg at my corner

folded under the pressure of the eight blowing demons. I was forced to the ground as it toppled over. As I lay there on my back, the cake came careening down the tilted table. Before I could lift a hand to deflect it, the beautifully decorated birthday cake slid across my blouse. Its final resting place was a spot just under my chin, with the gooey icing plastering my face, neck, and ears!

My one hope, that this was all a terrible nightmare from which I would soon wake up, was dashed when the sound of Bitsey's voice penetrated my icing-filled ears.

"Mommy! Daddy! Look what Ernie did! Ernie ate all my burpday cake! Bad old Ernie! Bad old Ernie!"

CHAPTER SEVEN

"Hi, Mr. Tubb," Louise said as she very carefully climbed into the backseat of our car. "Hi, Ernie."

"Hi, Louise," we chorused.

"Hi, Wheeze," said a voice from the front seat.

"Oh, gosh, Bitsey . . . I didn't see you. Hi."

"Oh, Louise, that's a new skirt, isn't it? I just love it," I said as Dad pulled away from the curb.

"Thanks, Ernie. Mom got it for me. She said I shouldn't go to my very first dance without something new to wear."

I glanced at Dad to see if this bit of information had registered, but it didn't seem to get any reaction from him. I thought I'd direct his attention by saying, "Boy, Louise, that sure was *nice* of your mom."

"Say 'hi' to Bama," came the command from the front seat.

"Bitsey," I said, in my sternest older sister voice, "you should *never* interrupt when someone else is talking."

"But Wheeze didn't say 'hi' to Bama."

"Oh, for heaven's sake," I sighed, rolling my eyes at Louise. She gave me a wink, leaned over the back of the front seat and said, "Hi, Bama. How are you today?"

A squeaky voice answered, "Just fine, sank you."

In case you are wondering who or what or why this Bama is, there's a simple explanation. She is one of the many dollies, the favorite one, that Bitsey got for her birthday. But isn't that an unusual name for a doll? No . . . not if you can follow the twisted thinking pattern of my little sister. You see, the doll is wearing a yellow dress. You still don't make the connection. Well, little wonder. Actually, you should be a little concerned if you *did* make the connection. The key word is "yellow." Yellow as in yellow banana . . . little miss mystery-mouth's favorite fruit . . . which she calls "bamas." So now you see!

"Well, well, girls . . . it's your first dance," Dad began. A shiver went up my spine. I feared that this was the beginning of another one of his less-than-inspiring speeches.

He went on, "I bet both of you are really excited."

"Thank goodness," I thought, as a wave of relief swept over me.

"Oh, Dad, it's not *really* a dance."

"Bama can dance."

I ignored the dance queen and said, "You know it's just the dance *lessons* that the Squat P.T.A. offer every year."

"Now look, Ernie, you're going to a gym and there's going to be music, and couples are going to dance . . . I'd call that a dance."

"Oh, Dad!"

I looked at Louise and sighed. Actually we were about ready to die from excitement. We'd been talking about it for weeks and could hardly wait for tonight.

"BAMA CAN DANCE!"

The pronouncement was punctuated by an upside-down Bama shooting up from the front seat and bouncing up and down on her head.

"Well," Dad said, not willing to concede a bit, "I know that the two of you are going to have a super time at this whatever-you-want-to-call-it that I call a dance."

By now, we had arrived at the school.

"I'll be in the parking lot at 8:30 *sharp*," Dad said as Louise and I got out of the car.

"Okay, Dad. Thanks."

"Thanks, Mr. Tubb."

As the car pulled away from the curb, we heard the wail of, "Bama wanna go to the dance! Bama wanna dance!"

I muttered, "Bye bye, Bama," as we turned to go into the school building.

"She's so funny," Louise laughed.

I was about to point out just how *unfunny* Bitsey is but before I could, a familiar voice hooted, "Hey, hey, hey . . . if it isn't the famous Dancing Duo."

"How great, how wonderful," I moaned, "wouldn't you know we'd be greeted right at the front door by old megaphone-mouth."

"Just ignore him, Ernie," advised Louise.

"Easier said than done," I said through clenched teeth. I knew Louise was right though.

"Hey, Al . . . you ever heard of the famous Dancing Duo?"

"Gosh, Murph, if you mean Awkward Annie and Graceless Gloria, I sure have," chimed in the mouth's dumb friend.

"No, no . . ." Murphy brayed. "it's *Dumbo* and *Dodo*, the two dancing *elephants*. Everyone's heard of them."

"Talk about *Dumbos*," I said to Louise.

She nodded and we left the idiots who were almost hysterical with what they thought was their own cleverness. Ellie motioned for us to join her over on one side of the gym.

"Hi, Ernie . . . hi, Louise. I'm sure you were subjected to the official predictably-obnoxious greeters at the door."

"Those two nitwits . . . how can they think they're so funny?" I asked.

"I was hoping they wouldn't come to the dance lessons," Ellie said, expressing the hope we all had had.

"Well, I absolutely and positively *refuse* to dance with either of them," I stated. "They can kick me out of this dance class if they want to, but I will *not* dance with either one of those two bozos!"

"Me neither!" Ellie declared.

Louise, always the thoughtful one, said, "Well, you know we might have to . . . but it would only be for one dance."

The thought sickened me. I retorted, "I don't care if it's only for half-a-dance . . . no, make that one step of one dance . . . I simply will not do it!" I made my pronouncement loud and clear so that the rest of the little group of girls who had drifted over to stand with us could hear me. Lisa poked me in the arm and said, "I bet you don't feel that way about Mr. Dreamboat, do you?"

Lisa and I sit beside each other in English class and we had often discussed the "dreamboat" who sits in the row just ahead of us. His name is Tim Marshall and all of the girls are absolutely mad about him. He is so good-looking and really friendly, too . . . such a contrast to the big dumb-mouth. Tim was nice too, he never teased anyone like Murphy did.

We all sighed, happy just thinking about him. None of us even dared mention how it would be to dance with him.

"Oh my . . . oh, don't look now," breathed Ellie, "but guess who just walked in?"

The whole group of us turned as one, just in time to see Tremendous Tim enter with a group of boys. I really will never be able to understand why he would want to hang out with that stupid Murphy and his equally stupid pals.

"Oooooh," Ellie sighed dramatically as we all turned back, "someone will get to be *his* partner."

Lisa pretended to swoon, "I'll just *die* if he chooses me for his partner."

We were all giggling when a man's voice boomed out, "Will all of the young ladies and gentlemen please form a circle around Marge and me?"

We moved slowly toward the stage end of the gym where Mr. and Mrs. Step were standing. She was adjusting a tape recorder that was on the stage. He was busy smiling at all of us and attempting to organize the large circle of "young ladies and gentlemen."

The Steps owned and operated the Step Dance Studio in Pleasant Valley. It was, in fact, the only dance studio in town. They had been around for a long time, and I do mean a *very* long time. Why, would you believe it . . . my parents had been taught to dance by the Steps. So you see that they really have been here forever.

"Ah, good, very good."

Mr. Step was still encouraging us to gather closer. "Now boys . . . don't be bashful."

He grinned as he said this and most of us giggled, not because he was funny, but because we were all so nervous about our first lesson.

"Fine . . . a very fine circle. Now then," he continued, "we must all have a partner, no? Yes, yes . . . partners. A good thing for dancers."

Louise, Ellie, Lisa and I smiled nervously at each other, wondering just who this partner we must have would be.

Mr. Step continued, "Now we have a simple way in which to choose partners. Girls . . . you will all take two steps into the circle. Ah, very good. Now, girls again, face a counter-clockwise direction."

Wouldn't you know . . . clockwise and counter-clockwise always get me confused, so of course, naturally, I turned in the wrong direction. I found myself staring at Lisa. From across the circle came the comment, "Count on old Ernie being *backwards* again."

Several of dumbhead's buddies began to laugh, but were stopped short by a glance from Mr. Step.

"Good grief," I thought, "Murphy never misses anything that he can tease me about."

"Now boys, it is your turn. You will all face clockwise, the opposite direction. Ah . . . good, very good. When Marge starts the music you will all walk in the direction you are facing. Continue walking until the music stops. The person you are next to then will be your partner for the first dance. Simple, no?

47

Yes. Does everyone understand?"

I had often played musical chairs when I was little, but this was the first time I ever played musical steps.

As we all nodded, I thought, "If John Murphy stops next to me I will keep on walking. I will walk out of this gym and not stop until I get home."

"Gower . . . oh, Gower," called Mrs. Step.

"Yes, Marge?"

"Gower, don't forget to remind them to walk normally . . . and not to bump into the person in front of them."

"Yes, yes, of course. As Marge just said, walk as normally as you would . . . let's say . . . in school."

I noticed he gave the boys a look as he said this. Murphy must have come up with another dumb crack because the boys near him laughed.

The music began and the two circles rotated looking like two wheels going in the opposite direction. Louise and Lisa were ahead of me and Ellie was right behind me. As we passed, most of the boys either smiled or looked down at their feet. Old loud-mouth had to be different, though. I braced myself for some stupid comment as I passed him. My expectation was fulfilled.

"Hey, Al, this must be a circus parade . . . it's the march of the elephants."

I was just relieved that the music hadn't stopped at that moment. I was wondering what unfunny thing he would say the second time we passed when the music suddenly did stop. I almost bumped into Lisa.

"Now turn and face your partner," said Mr. Step enthusiastically. "Simple, yes? Yes."

When I turned I thought I would faint dead away. There, facing me, actually smiling at me with his gorgeous movie-star smile, was Tim. I was stunned.

"Looks like you're stuck with me," he said.

Stuck with him ... with Tim ... with Mr. Dreamboat. I couldn't imagine anything better in the whole world than to be stuck with him. I knew every other girl in the gym would love to be "stuck" with Tim.

Little did I know then, Tim was not only gorgeous he was also quite adept at foretelling the future. The very moment he uttered those words, "stuck with me," I should have polite-ly excused myself saying "no, thank you, I do not care to have you as my partner," rushed home, hurried through my room, and locked myself safely in my closet. Did good old unsuspect-ing Ernie do any of these things? No, of course not. I realized I was the envy of all of the other girls and was nearly dying from happiness. In truth, I was beginning to feel a bit faint. Then I understood why ... I was holding my breath as I gaz-ed at Tim. As I quickly gulped in some air, Mr. Dreamboat reached out his hand and grasped mine. A shiver went down my back.

"Now, young ladies and gentlemen, watch as Marge and I do the following steps. We are beginning with a simple two-step then we will go on to the more complicated dances."

The Steps demonstrated first without the music, then with it. It was almost more than I could do to concentrate on the dance movements with Terrific Tim holding my hand. I couldn't help but see that we were the only partners holding hands.

"Oh," I thought dreamily, "he's so neat. I'm so lucky."

The music stopped.

"Now I want all of you to try the dance. Do just as Marge and I did," instructed Mr. Step.

The music started again, I looked at Tim. Tim smiled again, stepped closer, and then . . . then he actually put his arm around my waist. We began to dance the two-step. Then it came to me . . . I had died and gone to heaven. No . . . heaven was yet to come. As we danced, Tim touched his head to mine. *Then* I was in heaven. I fervently hoped that the music would never stop . . . that we'd spend the rest of our entire lives just this way.

"Oh, please," I begged, "please don't let me step on his feet. I'll be nice to Bitsey forever if only I don't step on his feet."

There we were . . . dancing . . . head touching head. I knew that every one of the other girls was dying to change places with me. I should have let one of them do it. But no, I was so happy that I didn't even care that Tim was chewing what must have been a very large wad of gum.

"Chomp, chomp, pause. Chomp, chomp, pause," sounded in my ear.

"Isn't that just like him," I thought. "Chewing to the beat of the music. He *is* perfect."

That's the way I felt as long as the music went on. It was *after* the music stopped that I came crashing back into the normal harsh world of Ernestine Cecelia Tubb. When the music stopped, I felt a strong tug on my head.

I momentarily thought, "Well, isn't that strange! What on

earth could be pulling at my hair?"

That's when I heard Tim gasp, "Oh, no," and the tugging on my hair stopped.

I looked at him to see what was the matter. he stared at me open-mouthed and said, "Oh, Ernie . . . I'm sorry. I didn't mean to . . . please don't be mad. Oh, Ernie."

Since I figured our dance had been absolute perfection, I couldn't understand why he was taking on so.

Then Louise said, "Oh, Ernie . . . oh, my . . . Ernie, Ernie!"

I was becoming concerned since more and more of the kids were beginning to look at me.

"What's the matter? Louise? Tim?"

Louise answered, "It's your hair." Then she just stood there looking upset, but not saying any more.

"Well, what about my hair?"

I don't mind telling you I was getting more than just a little annoyed by their reactions. Tim's bothered me the most. He looked as if he was about to pass into a catatonic state.

It was then that I, along with every other occupant of the gym, heard Megaphone-Mouth loudly proclaim, "Hey, hey, hey . . . nobody can say that Tim isn't stuck on Ernie."

A roar of laughter erupted. I could just barely hear Louise say, "Ernie . . . your hair . . . Tim's gum . . . it's stuck in your hair. It's all twisted around in there!"

CHAPTER EIGHT

Luckily for me, our infamous dance lesson was on a Wednesday night. You may wonder how I can consider anything at all "lucky" about that night . . . well, it's just that there were only two days of school left in which I had to endure the endless and unfunny "gum in your hair" jokes. Thanks mainly to that great broadcaster of disaster, John Murphy, the news had spread like wildfire throughout the entire school by the time I arrived on Thursday. I am quite sure that everybody, including the school custodians, spent the day having a good laugh on poor old Ernie. Students I barely knew stopped to make some comment to the girl with the lop-sided head. Yes . . . sadly enough, that's right . . . lop-sided. You see, the only way to remove chewed-into-your-hair gum is to *cut* it out. Even though Mom did her best to keep me from looking like a freak when she cut it, when Tim chews gum, he *really* chews.

After combing and brushing my hair at least one hundred ways and trying countless styles, I simply resigned myself to the fact that no matter what I did, my hair looked like it had just been blown-dry with a mixmaster.

When Friday came, I thought things couldn't get any worse and I was looking forward to a quiet weekend. Well, as I've said before, I'll never be able to make a living on my ability to foretell the future. Things did get worse . . . much worse . . . that very afternoon. It all began at cheerleading practice after school.

We had just finished one of our cheers and Mrs. Volumous was praising us for our good work.

"Girls, that last cheer was just perfect. You're simply going to wow them next week at our first game."

Cindy, still panting from the exertion of the last cheer, said, "Mrs. V."

"Yes, Cindy?"

"Mrs. V. . . . I've got a great idea. It would make us look even better. I was talking to my cousin who's a cheerleader at St. Michael's School in Florida. She told me their squad has a mascot. And . . . well . . . don't you think it would be a super idea if we had one?"

"Oh, that sounds just *divine*," Carla chimed in.

Louise and I exchanged smiles. We had decided that Carla was going through her "divine" stage. She was unable to say one sentence without using that word. Last year her word was "awesome."

"Just what kind of mascot did you have in mind, Cindy?" asked our coach.

"Well, my cousin said that a little sister of one of the girls was theirs. She even wore a uniform just like the cheerleaders."

Several of the girls were getting excited about the prospect. Brenda asked, "Gosh . . . would there be time before our first game to find someone?"

Mrs. Volumous laughed, "First we have to decide, then find someone."

"Oh, it would be absolutely *divine* to have a mascot," sighed you-know-who.

I wasn't too sure just how divine having a mascot would be, but it did sound like a good idea.

"Now," said Mrs. Volumous, "which of you has a little sister who might want to be our mascot?"

I looked around the group, but no hand went up. Then Brenda said, "I have a little sister, but she's too little. We'd have to change diapers if we used her."

Everyone laughed and we continued looking at one another. It never entered my head that Louise would do what she did next. She looked at me with a grin, then raised her hand. All of a sudden I had a sinking feeling in the pit of my stomach.

"Mrs. V. I know *just* the little girl. She would be fabulous. She's so cute *and* she has already seen all of the cheers."

I didn't know how to stop what was coming. I had a momentary impulse to stuff one of my pom-pons into Louise's mouth, but I knew it was too late. I broke out in a cold sweat as I stood there, unable to avert what I knew would be a catastrophe.

Louise went on, seemingly unaware of my reaction, "It's Ernie's little sister, Bitsey."

"How old is Bitsey, Ernie?" asked Mrs. Volumous.

I couldn't even answer her. I thought I was suffering so much from shock I might never speak again.

"How could she?" I thought. "How could Louise, who used to be my very best friend, do this to me?"

The instigator of the soon-to-be-realized disaster gave me a funny look, then answered for me, "Bitsey's four years old. She just had her fourth birthday and she'd be absolutely perfect."

"Oh . . . what a *divine* name," came from you-know-who again.

Mrs. Volumous looked at me, "Ernie?"

Finally regaining my power of speech, I croaked, "Oh . . . I don't think . . . I don't think she could do it."

"And why is that?" asked Mrs. Volumous.

I hesitated, knowing I couldn't declare the real reason, "Because she's such a ding-bat."

I obviously hesitated too long because Louise stepped in again, saying, "Of course she could. She's really cute. She does the cheers with us when we practice in Ernie's backyard."

Cute! All of the many embarrassing moments she had caused me crossed my mind at that instant . . . so many I couldn't begin to count them. All of them due to "cute" little Bitsey! The only excuse I could think of, lame as it was, was, "Oh, I'm sure my parents won't allow her to be a mascot."

"Sure they will," asserted Louise, looking at me in a puzzled way. I don't know why it was so hard for her to understand my resistance to the idea.

"Well," said Mrs. Volumous, "you can ask them after practice today, Ernie. We do need to know right away to get a uniform ready by game time."

I prayed that Louise would not pipe up and tell everyone that my *father* could get Bitsey's outfit done in plenty of time. I don't want the whole world to know that he does all of the sewing for us, even though he's great at it. It must have worked, for the only additional bit of information she felt compelled to add was, "Ernie's mother's picking us up after practice. We can ask her then."

I could tell by the way the others looked that they really were excited about the idea. It wouldn't do me any good to protest.

Mrs. Volumous said, "Fine. I'll walk out with you and we'll get the matter settled today — one way or the other."

One way or the other — a dark cloud settled over my head for the remainder of our practice time. I knew there would be only *one* way for things to go. Bitsey the mascot spelled trouble — big trouble — for her sister Ernie . . . that much I could count on. Just how it would happen or when I didn't know . . . but it would happen, that I did know. It was almost enough to make me quit the squad then and there. As it turned out, that would have been the best thing I could have done. The one slim hope that I had, and slim it was, was that Mom would say no. I was still clinging to that hope when Louise, Mrs. Volumous and I walked down the sidewalk to our waiting car. Mom was picking us up on her way home from the hardware store so the "cute, adorable little sister mascot" wasn't in the car. I had that to be thankful for, at least.

Louise and I climbed into the car as Mrs. Volumous called, "Hello there, Mrs. Tubb."

Mom, with a questioning look on her face, replied, "Why, hello. I hope nothing is wrong."

"Oh, no . . . nothing at all. Actually I've just come out to ask you for a big favor. My cheerleaders . . . and I . . . think it would be a great idea to have a mascot for the squad. Ernie's little sister sounds perfect. We were hoping you would permit her to do it."

Mom turned her head to look directly at me. As I managed a weak smile I sent thought waves to her, "No . . . no . . . say no . . . absolutely not . . . no . . . no . . . no!" I can tell you right now that there's nothing to this business of mental telepathy.

Mom turned back to our coach and told her, "Why, I suppose so. I don't see why not. I will have to ask Bitsey, though."

My last hope vanished. I knew the little pest would go wild with excitement at the first mention of it.

"Of course," agreed Mrs. Volumous. "If she does want to do it, she'll have to have an outfit made like the ones the cheerleaders wear."

"Oh, that's no problem at all. My husband can whip one up in nothing flat!"

"Great. Ernie can give me the verdict on Monday then. Nice talking with you, Mrs. Tubb."

"Thank you. It's always a pleasure to see you. The girls think so much of you. We do appreciate all of the time you spend with them."

"Oh, I love it. Have a nice weekend."

"Bye, Mrs. V.," Louise called as Mom started the car. I just sat there, too upset to say anything at all. My last hope had vanished . . . I knew I was doomed!

CHAPTER NINE

The voice amplified by the loud-speaker boomed out. "It's a first down for the Squat Squires!"

We were all screaming and jumping up and down because our football team was very close to making the first touchdown of the game.

"Quick," hollered Brenda, "let's do the touchdown cheer."

The Squat Squad rushed to line up and begin the chant.

"We want a touchdown. We want a touchdown."

"Move over, Bitsey," I hissed.

"We want a touchdown. We want a touchdown."

"I said . . . *move over*, Bitsey!"

As you may have guessed, my dear sweet little sister, that "cute, adorable, absolutely perfect" mascot, was standing so close to me that I could barely move, let alone do the touchdown chant. Yes, Bitsey had gladly accepted the role of mascot . . . not without some confusion on her part, though. When Mom asked her if she wanted to be the cheerleaders' mascot, she asked, "What's a masked cot, Mommy?" Once Mom explained just exactly what a "masked cot" would be doing, her face lighted up like a Roman candle. She immediately kicked a foot in the air and yelled, "Gimme a cow. Gimme a piggy." Mom looked at Dad, who was laughing as hard as she was, and said, "Well, I guess that means yes!" Thus it was settled, much to my dismay.

So here I stood in front of hundreds of Squat students, trying to maintain the dignity of a junior high school cheerleader and, at the same time, cope with the little ding-bat hollering, "We wanna bunch-a-clowns" while pointing in the wrong direction.

"Bitsey," I hissed between my teeth again, "if you don't move over and give me some room *and* point the other way, I'll . . ."

"Touchdown!" boomed the loud-speaker voice.

"Yeah!" screamed the cheerleaders. Everyone in the grand-stands leaped up and yelled and screamed with us. Then a hush fell over the crowd as our team got ready to kick for the extra point. Suddenly Bitsey's shrill voice pierced the silence as she cried out loud and clear, "We wanna bunch-of-clowns."

I couldn't believe it, I simply could not. I mean to tell you, I thought I would *die*. I wanted to die. The entire grandstand erupted with laughter. I turned to the other cheerleaders, knowing how upset they would be and I was stunned! They were all, and I do mean all, looking at Bitsey and laughing.

"Doesn't that just figure," I thought. "Little mixed-up mouth messes up our cheer and everyone thinks she's so funny, so cute. Well, not me. Boy, oh boy, not me!"

The laughing turned into cheers as the football spiraled between the goal posts. We had made the extra point.

"Thank goodness," I thought. "Now maybe the 'bunch-a-clowns' will be forgotten."

I should have know better, I really should have. As soon as the cheering subsided John (the great bench-warmer) Murphy turned around and, looking directly at me, said loudly, "Hey, hey, hey . . . Bitsey and Bozo do it again."

"Oh, how wonderful," I thought. "Thanks to the two loud-mouths I'll spend the remainder of my years at Squat known as Bozo the clown!"

Then Louise came through with a remark that made me forgive her—almost—for suggesting Bitsey as our mascot. She took a couple of steps towards the bench and hollered, "Watch out for splinters, John."

I flashed her a smile of appreciation amid the general laughter . . . for once at Murphy's expense.

Brenda asked, "Mrs. V., would it be alright to try our 'V for Victory' cheer during the next time out?"

Brenda was our captain but Mrs. Volumous had said she would help us out at our first appearance and was sitting close by in the grandstands.

"Well, I don't know," she answered slowly. "We did just learn it yesterday. Are you sure you all know it well enough?"

"Oh yes," gushed Lisa.

There was a chorus of yeses from several of the other girls and Carla added her usual, "It would be *divine*, Mrs. V."

"I wanna do it," chimed in you-know-who.

"Bitsey," I said warningly.

"I wanna do the TV cheer!" demanded the sweet little mascot.

"We really do know how to do it," Brenda pleaded.

"Well, okay girls. But it's a bit tricky, you know."

"Oh, we won't have any trouble at all," I added. Once again proving I'll never have any success at foreseeing the future.

The 'V for Victory' cheer was our favorite cheer even though we had just learned it. The reason we liked it so much was that we formed a pyramid — a human pyramid. Three of us, Brenda, Lisa, and I were the bottom layer, kneeling on our hands and knees. Louise and Carla then climbed up on our backs, also on their hands and knees. Then, Melissa, the smallest of us, climbed up to stand on their backs just as we finished by chanting V-I-C-T-O-R-Y. We were very proud *and* excited about our ability to do this cheer. We had watched the high school cheerleaders do it and couldn't wait to show off.

Finally, after what seemed forever, the other team called a time out. The Squat Squad sprang into action, running to our starting positions. Everyone, of course, except our darling little mascot, who had absolutely no part in the "V for Victory" cheer. All she was to do was to stand off to one side, but she couldn't even remember to do that. Just as Brenda was ready to give us our signals, little Miss Confusion bumbled through our starting formation loudly crying, "I forget!"

"Over there," I said, pointing to the side.

"What?"

"Oh, for heaven's sake, Bitsey." I was trying to keep a smile on my face as Mrs. Volumous had said we should. "Go over there . . . over to that side . . . and just stand there. And keep your mouth shut."

"Where?"

I couldn't help it. I completely lost patience with her.

I shouted, "OVER THERE!"

Bitsey was about to say something else when Louise told her, "Bitsey, honey, the cheerleading mascot gets to hurry over to that side and help us by *watching* this cheer."

Bitsey turned on her heels immediately and hot-footed it out of our way.

"Louise sure is a marvel with her," I thought. I hoped we still had plenty of time to complete our cheer as Brenda signaled to begin.

"V-I-C-T-O-R-Y!" we yelled as Brenda, Lisa and I knelt down to form the first layer of our pyramid. I was feeling pretty nervous since I had the important middle spot. Mrs. Volumous had said that I would be responsible for the stability of the whole pyramid.

We continued to yell, "We're the best team because we try!"

Carla and Louise climbed onto our backs.

"Ooooff," moaned Lisa.

"Sorry," apologized Carla as her other knee jabbed me in the back.

The cheer continued, "We're the Squires from Squat Junior High!"

At this point, Melissa climbed up to the top. Slowly as we finished with "V-I-C-T-O-R-Y," she stood up straight, her feet firmly planted on Carla and Louise.

The crowd began to cheer wildly.

"Wow," I can remember thinking seconds before the disaster struck, "the crowd really *loves* our victory cheer."

Now I really should have known better. I mean, how often have you ever seen a grandstand filled with people give a standing ovation for a cheer. I'd say never, right? So why did I think they were cheering for us? I guess it's just due to my optimistic nature, my tendency to look on the bright side of life. I began suspecting something was wrong, though, when the cheers changed to moans and loud yells of concern. I have only a vague recollection of hearing Mrs. Volumous call a warning before an enormous force struck me to the ground. You must remember my important position to the pyramid . . . the stabilizing middle girl . . . the now soon-to-be-crushed cheerleader.

"Yeow!" Melissa screamed from far over my head.

Immediately after, the human pyramid was transformed into a moaning, groaning sea filled with twisted arms and legs.

Mrs. Volumous had rushed over to untangle us.

"Girls . . . girls . . . are you alright? Is anyone hurt? Oh, dear . . . Melissa, are you alright? Louise? Brenda? Ernie? Be careful . . . maybe you shouldn't move. Here, let me help.

By some miracle none of us were injured in our unplanned tumble to the ground.

"My," I thought as someone lifted me up, "I'm quite sure the Squat Squad's first performance of the 'V for Victory' cheer will not be soon forgotten."

It was then that I noticed it . . . the enormous force that pushed me flat. The game football was on the ground right next to the scene of destruction. As I looked around, I saw that all of the football players, coaches and referees were standing there . . . staring in utter disbelief. Evidently the cheerleaders had run out of time . . . as well as out of luck.

The hushed atmosphere was shattered by the sing-song chant

CHAPTER TEN

"Hey, hey, hey . . . there's a bunch of clowns . . . about to take on some pounds," hooted the big-mouth as he walked past us in the cafeteria. Murphy and his dumb friends seemed to think his stupid comment was absolutely hilarious. Even though it had been two weeks since the 'V for Victory' disaster, Murphy kept up his idiotic teasing. Every time he saw us . . . any of us . . . anywhere, he made the same inane comment.

Louise, Lisa, Brenda and I were standing in line for food. Louise advised, "Just ignore them."

"Oh . . . they make me so *mad*," Brenda complained.

"Me too," I said, "but Louise is right. Believe me, we know all about John Murphy from being with him in elementary school all those years . . . those long, horrible years."

"Well, I just don't know how you tolerated him all that time," Lisa commented.

"We didn't have any other choice," I said, Louise nodded in agreement.

Just then, Carla came over to say, "I'm sitting over by the window. I have some simply *divine* seats saved for you."

"Okay. Good. We'll be right over," Lisa told her.

"*Divine.*"

She hurried back to guard our claim.

"Oh, yummie . . . pizza," crowed Brenda.

"Yuk," I said. "How can you eat that cardboard stuff they call pizza here at Squat?"

"Oh, I think it's really good," she said, helping herself to a pizza plate.

"Hi, Melissa, what do you recommend today?" asked Lisa.

Melissa looked at Brenda and laughed, "Well . . . anything but the pizza."

Brenda, pretending to be insulted, sniffed, "Oh, the rest of you just don't know what's good."

"Thank goodness it's not the only choice," Lisa said, reaching for the hamburger plate.

I took one also and we moved down the line.

"Gosh, look at that," said Louise, "peas again. Mr. Sumkins must have a huge pea patch!"

"Whoever heard of the combinaton of pizza and peas?" Brenda asked.

"Maybe it's 'p' day," I suggested.

I was met with blank looks, so I explained, "Look at the dessert . . . pudding."

More blank looks.

I went on, "Well, don't you see . . . pizza, peas, pudding. They all begin . . ."

The rest of my explanation was drowned out by their groans.

"I think Mrs. Yummers is having too much of an effect on ou Ernie," laughed Louise as we walked toward our table.

Lisa agreed, "Sure . . . that must be it. Right Ernie?"

Brenda, with a twinkle in her eye, teased, "Oh, I don't think it's Mrs. Yummers who's having an effect on her."

I knew what was coming, but actually, I didn't mind.

Brenda went on, "As a matter of fact . . . it's Terrific Tim!"

Everyone laughed as Brenda explained, "He's in our home ec class, you know."

The others chorused, "We know . . . we know. You've told us at least a hundred times."

I could feel my face flushing as I said, "He *is* dreamy, but I don't think we'll ever dance together again."

Suddenly, I felt something hit the back of my neck. I reached my hand up and found a squashed pea. When I jerked my head around, I saw that Murphy and his pals were grinning like lunatics.

"Here we go again," I moaned.

Carla said, "I think we ought to tell the monitor. He's always trying to spoil our *divine* lunches."

I snorted, "A lot of good *that* does!"

Lisa agreed, "Yeah, it only made them worse the last time we did it.

"Oh, oh," Carla bubbled, "Look, look, look. Here comes that *divine* dreamboat himself."

We were all momentarily distracted as Tim walked by our table to join that of the dumbheads.

"Hi there, Ernie," he called, giving me that movie-star smile again.

"Oh . . . ah . . . hi," I managed to squeak as my face turned a deeper shade of red.

Trancelike, we all watched as he carried his tray the short distance to the other table.

"Oh, Ernie," Louise said, "he really *does* like you."

I hoped she was right. I wanted to be the one that Tim Marshall liked better than anyone else in the whole school . . . the whole world, even. I thought I should make some kind of denial though and said, "Oh, Louise, he does not. He just feels bad about chewing the gum into my hair."

That brought everyone's attention to my head. Lisa observed, "At least your hair has grown enough so you can't see where the gum was cut out."

"Yeah, what a relief," I said.

Just then a straw wrapper flipped into Brenda's pizza. We all turned and stared our meanest stares at the stupids. Murphy had such a wide smirk on his face I thought it would split . . . and wished it would.

"There has to be something we can do to get even with that big dumb ox," I muttered.

"Yeah, we'll have to get him," Brenda said, fishing the straw wrapper out of her plate. "We shouldn't have to put up with his silly nonsense day after day."

"You're right," Louise agreed, "but what can we do?"

Lisa slapped her hand down on the table and laughed, "Oh, I know, I know. I have it . . . the perfect way to get him!"

"What? How?" we all asked.

She motioned for us to bring our heads closer so she could whisper her plan. When she finished, Carla breathed, "Oh, how wonderful. Why, it's simply the most *divine* thing I ever heard."

Brenda looked doubtful, "Well, yeah . . . but will it work? A person would have to be pretty dumb to fall for that." Then, thinking about what she had just said, smiled, "It sure would work, wouldn't it?"

We all laughed and nodded.

Lisa added, "Well, it's really up to Melissa."

"What if she doesn't want to do it?" Louise asked.

"Oh, I think she will. Who do you think engineered it last year in our elementary school?"

"You're kidding," Brenda exclaimed. "Melissa?"

"Yep . . . all her idea. And it worked like a dream."

Lisa's smile was getting broader and broader. I loved the idea myself.

"Let's do it tomorrow," I said.

"Oh, Ernie, we can't," Lisa said. "Melissa has to have time to get the surprise . . . the Murphy special . . . ready. We'll do it Friday."

"Oh, of course . . . I didn't think of that," I replied. "But it's going to be hard to wait that long."

"Believe me, it will be worth it," Brenda assured me.

"We can talk to Melissa about it after cheerleading practice today," Louise said.

"Oh, isn't Friday going to be the most *divine* day!" gushed you-know-who.

"Yes," I said, "Friday is 'R-Day' . . . R for revenge."

Everytime we looked at one another that afternoon, we would break up thinking about our great "get-even-with-the-big-dumb-ox" plan.

*   *   *   *

"Hey, hey, hey . . . there's a bunch of clowns about to put on some pounds."

Friday had finally arrived. Melissa had gone along with the plan . . . very enthusiastically . . . and we were so excited we could hardly stand it. We had hurried to the cafeteria so we could get our trays and sit down before the victim and his buddies did. We wanted to have a good look at Murphy's face when he took his first taste of milk . . . milk especially prepared for him . . . the Murphy special.

As we sat down, Brenda asked, "Do you think Melissa can make absolutely sure that he gets the right container of milk?"

"Oh, sure," Lisa said confidently. "Don't worry . . . and Murphy can't suspect . . . or prove . . . a thing."

"Oh . . . I'm so nervous," Louise said.

I felt the same way, "So am I. There are actually butterflies in my stomach. Oh, Lisa . . . won't he suspect something when his milk is warm?"

"No . . . it won't be. Melissa put it back in the refrigerator yesterday."

Louise looked worried, "What if it didn't set out long enough?"

Lisa exclaimed, "Three days! That's plenty long enough as warm as it is."

"Oh, yes," Carla wrinkled her nose. "I took a drink of milk that had only been left out one day. It was anything but *divine*!"

Lisa shushed us then, saying "Here they come. Start eating. Try not to look nervous. Be normal."

"Hey, Al . . . the clowns must be hungry today . . . they don't even have time to chatter to each other."

His remark panicked us and we all began talking at once. He gave us a strange look, but kept going to his table.

"Boy, was that ever close," I said, "I hope we didn't make him suspicious."

Brenda glanced at their table, "No ... they're goofing around the way they always do."

She and I were facing the guys' table. The Mouth was sitting directly opposite us and we could see his every move. Brenda kept up a running commentary on his actions for the benefit of those who didn't have his face in view.

"He's shoving half of his fish sandwich into his mouth now."

"Boy, that should make him thirsty," giggled Lisa.

"*Divinely* thristy."

"Boy, I don't think I can stand this," I said.

Before anyone else could say anything, Brenda said, "Oh ... oh ... now! Here it comes! He's making a grab for his milk!"

We waited breathlessly.

"He's opening the carton."

Louise asked, "Does he look like he suspects anything?"

"No, he's just mouthing off to his friends, as usual."

"The motor-mouth's probably plotting some terrible thing to do to us," I said.

"He's got the wrapper off the straw. Look out, it's coming this way."

It landed on the floor near our table.

"Big dumb-ox," I said. "He's sure getting just what he deserves."

"Here he goes. The straw's in the carton. *Right now* he's tak-

71

ing a big drink of milk!"

At her words, "Right now," our whole table turned to look. Our plan worked beautifully. As Carla would say, our revenge was just *divine*. What we all . . . what everyone in the cafeteria . . . saw was John sitting there with a big mouthful of spoiled milk. But only for a moment. Then his eyes became as large as saucers and his face turned bright red. At the same time, he opened his mouth and spit out the milk in a violent geyser. I mean, he sprayed all of his stupid gang of buddies with the putrid milk.

A roar of laughter erupted that could very probably be heard in the principal's office.

No one at our table was able to contain herself. Tears were streaming down everyone's face and our sides ached. I knew we all wanted to congratulate each other, but that would have to wait until we were in a condition to talk again.

It was a day that I . . . that we all . . . would remember happily for a very, very long time. It was *divine*!

CHAPTER ELEVEN

". . . and those are the basic steps in making a chocolate cake," Mrs. Yummers said. "Now divide up into into your assigned pairs and start cooking!"

It was next to impossible for me to concentrate on Mrs. Yummers' instructions once I found out that my partner was to be the *dreamboat*. I just completely fell apart. All I could hope was that nothing would happen to embarrass me in front of Mr. Gorgeous. I looked over and noticed that Brenda was grinning at me. She gave me the thumbs-up sign just as a voice behind me said, "Well, Ernie, I bet the two of us can really cook up a fantastic chocolate cake."

The blood left my head. I was sure I was going to pass out that very instant. Imagine . . . the two of us . . . cooking together. Standing side by side . . . talking to each other. I figured I must have died and gone to heaven.

I turned and stared open-mouthed at Tim for a moment, then, trying to compose myself so I wouldn't seem like an utter fool to him, managed a weak, "Yeah . . . fantastic."

He smiled at me, "Well, we had better get started."

I cleverly responded, "Yeah."

"Let's see, we'll need a mixing bowl." He was looking in one of the cupboards.

"And a saucepan to melt the chocolate in." I had finally regained my power of speech.

I watched in silent admiration while Tim located a bowl and the saucepan.

"What else, Ernie?"

"Oh, ah, well . . . an electric beater."

"Oh, sure. Gosh, Ernie, you know so much. Why don't you get the ingredients while I look for the beater?"

I walked toward one of the refrigerators. He called after me, "Ernie, do you need any help?"

"Heavens, no, Tim," I laughed in what I hoped was a gracious way. "To do a simple job like this?"

I was soon to live to regret my overconfident manner.

"Okay. You do that while I try to figure out how to put the beaters on this handle."

"Let's see," I mused to myself, looking into the refrigerator, "We . . . my partner . . my dreamy partner . . . and I need eggs, milk and butter."

I repeated, "Eggs, milk and butter," taking three eggs out of a carton and trying to find the butter.

My sing-song continued as I tried to arrange the eggs in one hand to free the other for the bar of butter.

"There . . . eggs and butter. Now, milk, then back to *my* partner." A half-gallon of milk was on the top shelf.

"Hhmmm," I thought. "This may take some juggling."

I looked at the eggs I was holding in one hand and the bar

of butter in the other, then at the milk. I briefly wondered if I could balance the jug on my head, then decided not to try. I certainly didn't want to have an accident.

"Well, Ernie, don't just stand here," I told myself. "You have to think of some way to carry all of these things back in one trip. After all, you don't want Tim to think you're helpless, do you?"

Since I didn't have to answer that question, I concentrated on the problem. Then it came to me.

"Of course," I said. "So easy!"

I placed the eggs back in the carton, picked up the half-gallon of milk, and tucked it . . . sort of . . . under my left arm. With the butter in my right hand, I very carefully proceeded to pick up the three eggs, one at a time, with my left hand. I just managed to grasp the third egg with the tips of my fingers.

"There," I thought, as I shoved the refrigerator door shut with my back. "Tim will be so impressed."

I was certainly right there. Tim was really going to be impressed . . . but not in the way I meant him to be.

When I turned back, I saw that he was still fussing with the electric beater.

I stood and watched him, thinking, "Oh, he's so cute when he's concentrating that way."

Concentrating. That was the word. Concentrating on what he was doing. Which is what I should have been doing too . . . instead of gazing at him so adoringly.

Poor old unsuspecting Ernie, gingerly walking back to her perfect partner with whom she would make the perfect cake, was completely unaware of the soon-to-happen catastrophe.

75

Just as I walked by Diana, another seventh-grade chef, she let out a blood-curdling yell and jumped back from the range . . . right smack into me!

Mrs. Yummers came running, "Girls, girls . . . how many times have I warned you to be careful!"

Diana began whining, "My finger . . . the pan was hot and I burned my finger."

Mrs. Yummers took Diana's hand, "There . . . there . . . I'm sure it will be alright. Come along, dear, I'll put some ointment on it."

I couldn't believe it. Once again, I had become the invisible girl. I stood there, bravely clinging to what was left of our ingredients. Egg goo was splattered all over my skirt and dripping down my leg.

Did poor old Ernie whine and cry to get attention and sympathy like Diana? No, of course not. She just stood there, willing herself to disappear. Finally, Mrs. Yummers noticed my horrible condition. Horrible and pathetic.

"Oh, Ernie, for goodness sake . . . what happened? What did you do? How on earth did you make such a mess?"

What did *I* do? How did *I* make such a mess? Wouldn't you know . . . it always seemed to happen to me . . . the innocent bystander . . . blamed for something not her fault. Before I could explain, she went on, "Quick, somebody . . . get Ernie some paper towels."

Before I could say, "cracked egg," five handfuls of paper towels were thrust into my face. At about the same time someone took the milk and butter from my now immobile arms.

"Here, let me help," Brenda said, taking the paper towels

and sopping up that icky goo from my legs and skirt. I grabbed some more and tried to clean my hands. I looked down and saw that the runaway goo had stained my once sparkling sock with a dingy yellow.

Then I heard Tim's voice . . . right next to me.

"Oh, Ernie . . . that's too bad."

He took hold of my arm and said, "Here, let me get you back to our counter."

Suddenly, I could have been standing knee-deep in a vat of egg goo and cared less. Tim was concerned. Mr. Dreamboat was holding my arm. I felt faint once again.

"Oh, a little egg on my sock . . . that's nothing."

I smiled bravely at him. I heard Brenda mutter, "Oh, brother," as she set the milk down on the counter in front of us.

"Everybody back to work," Mrs. Yummers ordered. "Back to your cooking, everything's under control."

Diana was still whining, "My finger, Mrs. Yummers, it hurts so."

"Yes, yes, Diana. Come over to my desk. I always keep emergency supplies there, just in case we have a minor accident."

"It really burns," sniffled the invalid as she followed our teacher to her desk.

"Maybe she should be taken directly to the burn unit at St. Charles Hospital," I suggested.

Brenda, Tim, and I giggled and once again I was on top of the world. "I'll get more eggs, Ernie. You probably want to wash your hands."

As I stood at the sink washing my hands, I couln't keep a

silly smile from spreading over my face. I just couldn't. Terrific Tim. Tremendous Tim. Tim the dreamboat. Tim cared about Ernestine Cecelia Tubb. Life was wonderful. Life was beautiful. Nothing . . . certainly nothing as minor as a little egg goo could dampen my spirits today. Not as long as Tim . . . *my* Tim . . . was at my side.

As you know by now, when I'm wrong I am really wrong! But then how was I to know that a cataclysmic event was just waiting to happen.

Tim came back, "Here are the eggs."

"Maybe *you* had better crack them into the bowl, considering the effect I seem to have on eggs today."

"Okay, Ernie."

As he began to do so, I asked, "Tim, what temperature did Mrs. Yummers say the oven was supposed to be?"

He wrinkled his forehead in the cutest way, then said, "Oh, ah, I think she said . . . medium . . . whatever that means."

"Oh . . . that's around 350 degrees." I was happy to reveal this bit of knowledge. Thank goodness, I had helped Dad with baking cookies. I was able to sound like a real authority.

"Gosh, Ernie, how do you know that?"

I could see that Tim was impressed.

"Oh well, Tim, I do a lot of baking at home."

Actually my "lot of baking" consisted of helping Dad bake cookies about three times in all.

"Wow, that's super, Ernie. I'm sure glad I'm *your* partner. Boy, am I ever lucky."

"I'm sure glad I'm *your* partner" will doubtlessly go down as the most ridiculous phrase ever uttered in the history of the

Cecil T. Squat Junior High School. After what happened . . . though really not my fault . . . I would be the lucky one. Lucky, that is, if Tim would ever feel safe in the same room with me, let alone as my cooking partner.

"Ernie . . . why don't you beat the eggs since you're the old pro at cooking. I'll cut the chocolate so it will melt faster."

Now I should have stopped right then and explained to my poor unwary partner that I was not an "old pro" . . . not even a semi-pro . . . not even a teeny-tiny pro. Helping Dad bake cookies three times does not meet the qualifications for becoming a pro. What I was was a beginner, a novice. But did I do this? No. Did I explain to Tim? No. Did I warn him that I didn't know what I was doing? No. Did I tell him to be on his guard? No. Did I tell him that the cookies I helped Dad bake were so hard that a hammer and chisel were needed to break them apart? No. Did I tell him that when I get into a kitchen the safest place to be is out of the room and preferably out of the building? No.

What Ernie-the-would-be-chef did say was, "Sure, Tim. I'll take care of the eggs." And to make matters worse, added, "Cooking's really quite simple once you get the hang of it."

So the ever-so-lucky-Tim began unwrapping the chocolate as Ernie-the-expert-cook took over the electric beater . . . to be known ever after as Ernie's spray painter. I turned it on low and it started to hum nicely. I eased the eggs in ever so carefully. I have to admit that it sure did look as if I knew what I was doing. Actually, I had practically convinced myself . . . as well as Tim . . . that I *did* know what I was doing.

"There, that's done," Tim said. "Now what's next?"

"You can pour in a little milk," said Ernie-the-gourmet.

Tim opened the milk and began to pour.

"Just say when, Ernie."

"When," I said, and he stopped pouring immediately.

I was certainly enjoying my "old pro" status. With all of the authority I could muster, I told him, "Now, we have to turn the beaters on high so the mixture will become nice and fluffy."

"Sure, whatever you say, Ernie."

The hum of the beaters changed to a high-pitched whine. It was at this moment . . . the very moment when I was feeling the most confident . . . that it happened.

"Ernie," called Brenda, from her counter.

I didn't take my eyes away from the mixer for a minute. "Yes?"

"Ernie, look at this."

Now, you wouldn't think a little phrase like, "Ernie, look at this," would ruin a person's life, would you? But, as fate would have it, the trusting-always-trying-to-please-Ernie took her watchful eyes away from her work and turned to look at Brenda.

Before I could see whatever it was she wanted me to look at, Tim shouted, "Ernie . . . STOP . . . STOP!"

There were accompanying yells from all around the room. I felt something hit me on the back of the neck. I turned back to look at my cooking partner. He was covered with frothy egg-milk goo from head to toe. Everyone else, who had been within a radius of six feet had also been spray-painted a pale yellow when I had lifted the beaters partly out of the bowl as I turned.

Mrs. Yummers had rushed over to turn off the mixer while

I stood motionless, too stunned to do anything at all. All she could say was "Oh, class . . . oh, Ernie . . . how could you!!!"

CHAPTER TWELVE

As a result of the great cooking disaster I was dubbed Betty - the cracked cook - Crocker by big-mouth Murphy. I was so mortified that I went out of my way to avoid seeing Tim. I simply could not face him. During lunch on the following week, he stopped at our table every day. He was nice enough to try to joke about it, saying he figured I was - justifiably - getting even with him for his gum-in-the-hair trick. Even that didn't help. I still couldn't look at him. The cheerleaders found out about it from Brenda, but by then the whole school had heard anyway. It didn't even matter to me that they were just about rolling on the ground in their hysteria . . . all I could think about was what I'd done to Tim.

Fortunately, something else came along in a few days to divert everyone. Did I say fortunately? I would soon learn otherwise. Unfortunately would have been a better word.

It happened on Wednesday morning. Louise and I were chatting in homeroom when the bell sounded and the PA system was switched on for the morning announcements.

"And a good Wednesday morning to everyone."

Our captain's voice came through loud and clear.

"Today is a special day at Cecil T. Squat Junior High School. Now, I can just hear some of you asking what could be so special on a day in the middle of the week."

Several groans were heard in the classroom.

"Well, you curious people, I'll tell you. One hundred and fifty years ago today . . . I'll repeat . . . this very day . . . a small band of brave and courageous pioneers came into our virgin valley and chose to make it their home. In this small band of brave pioneers there was a young couple by the name of . . ."

There was a long pause. A very long pause. Just as I was beginning to wonder if Mr. Sumkins had forgotten the name of this unforgettable couple, he roared forth with, "Quincy and Queenie Squat!"

There was dead silence for about two seconds, then it began. First, a sort of low hum came rumbling down the hallways. The hum gained in momentum until it was recognizable laughter cascading through the entire building. It finally erupted into a deafening roar. Finally, it began to subside. We could hear Mr. Sumkins talking to someone.

"What's the matter, Gladys? What's all that noise?"

"I'm sure I can't say, Mr. Sumkins."

"Did something happen that we don't know about?"

"Your guess is as good as mine, Mr. Sumkins."

"Well, hurry and find out . . . I must carry on."

I heard a door close and Mr. Sumkins continued, "Yes, this very day . . . an important day . . . a day to put away in your memory books, boys and girls, students of Squat. And on this very important day, what do we have for lunch? Ah, yes, my, my . . . we will be having a choice of either hotdogs or a noodle casserole. The science club will meet today after school in Mr. De Popoffs's room. That is, room 201. All money must be turned in for . . ."

As his voice droned on, my mind wandered off on its own, only to brought back to reality when the bell rang for my first class.

Louise was waiting for me just outside the door.

"What did you think of all of that?" she asked.

I looked at her blankly and asked, "About what?"

"Weren't you listening?"

"You mean about Quincy and Queenie? Why?"

"No, no, I mean about the homecoming."

"Homecoming? What homecoming? I didn't hear anything about any homecoming."

"You can sure get lost in your thoughts, Ernie. Betcha I know who you were thinking about," Louise teased.

"Oh, Louise . . . I don't think about Tim very much . . . hardly at all."

"Yeah . . . sure. Anyway . . . the high school homecoming."

"What about it?"

Louise filled me in on all of the details of Mr. Sumkins' announcement as we walked down the hall together.

"The parade at half-time sounds just great," I told her.

"Oh, doesn't it," she gushed. "And Ernie . . . oh, Ernie . . . just think . . . Nick . . . Nick will be there!"

Nick was the lifeguard we met on our vacation at Lake Kickapoo last summer . . . an older version of Tremendous Tim. In fact, Louise and I had called him, "Mr. Beautiful." He had told us he was on the high school football team, so that made the thought of going to the homecoming game all the more exciting.

"Great. We can all go together. Louise, do you think Nick will remember us?"

"Oh, I'm sure he'll remember you, Ernie."

I had a momentary flashback to a certain embarrassing incident. My shorts had split up the side during a limbo contest and Nick had been there to witness the whole humiliating event.

"We'll have a really great time," Louise said.

By then we had reached my next classroom, so I just told her, "Sure . . . we'll talk about it later . . . at lunch. See you."

Louise waved and went on to her class.

Well, we certainly did talk about it during lunch. In fact, it was the *only* topic of conversation. Even the big-mouth and his group were so busy talking among themselves they didn't have time to pester us. Of course, every now and then, one would let go with a raucous laugh and look over at us.

"Now, just what do you suppose those idiots are talking about?" Lisa asked, glancing at their table.

"Beats me," Louise answered. "At least they're leaving us alone today."

"You can be sure of one thing, though," Brenda commented, "they're up to no good."

"Right," I said, "and you know that it's no good for us! Especially if it has anything to do with the homecoming."

Our excitement reached new heights when we got to cheerleading practice and heard what Mrs. Volumous had to

85

tell us.

"Girls, I have something to ask you . . . a favor. We have been asked to ride on one of the homecoming floats during the half-time parade. I said I would check with you first be. . ."

Anything else she was going to say was cut off by our cheers and yells. When we quieted down to a roar, she laughed, "Well, I guess this means you're willing to do it."

That started the yells and shouts all over again. The only word I could make out through the din was "divine."

Lisa shouted, "Mrs. V."

"Yes, Lisa?"

We quieted down so we could hear Lisa's question.

"Mrs. V., what float will we be riding on?"

"Well, I don't have all of the details yet, but the high school cheerleading coach, who just happens to be a good friend of mine, has asked us to join her cheerleaders on their float."

Brenda and Carla called, at the same time, "Mrs. V."

"No more questions, girls, I really don't know any more than what I have already told you. I'll know more after I talk to Margie . . . Miss Moore, that is . . . the other coach."

When practice ended, Louise and I raced to our waiting car.

"Guess what, Dad!"

I started talking even before I got into the car.

Bitsey hollered, "Hi, Ernie . . . hi, Wheeze."

"Hi, Bitsey. Hi, Mr. Tubb."

"Hi, girls. My goodness, but you're excited. What on earth happened?"

"Oh, Dad, you'll never guess!"

"Nobody said hi to Bama."

I ignored the little creep, but of course Louise wouldn't.

"Hi, Bama," she said.

As Dad pulled the car away from the curb, he looked into the rear-view mirror and said, "Well, whatever this is, it must be good news."

"Oh, yes, Mr. Tubb. Just wonderful news."

I was about ready to burst with excitement as I said, "You know, Dad, the high school's homecoming is next week."

"What's a combhumming?"

"It's called a *homecoming*, Bitsey, and it's a very special football game that has a parade."

Dad half turned his head around to look at me, "Ernie, do you feel alright?"

"Oh, Dad! We are . . . we cheerleaders . . . we are going to *ride* in the high school homecoming parade!"

"Isn't that the greatest!" Louise added as we crossed the intersection and headed down her street.

"Well, girls, that is wonderful news."

"BITSEY WANNA RIDE IN THE COMBHUMMING PARADE!"

"Bitsey, honey," Dad said as he stopped the car in front of Louise's house, "I'm sure you will. After all, it's the cheerleaders who have been chosen and you're the mascot."

My feeling of elation began to wither and dry up at the thought of Bitsey on the float with us. What Ernestine Cecelia Tubb should have decided right then and there was to make a vow *not* to go to the homecoming. But no . . . not good old Ernie. Oh no, being the eternal optimist, I totally ignored those inner warnings. I totally ignored the possibility . . . the prob-

bability . . . the certainty . . . that a great disaster was hanging over my head, just waiting to happen.

CHAPTER THIRTEEN

"I'll be back to pick you girls up at exactly nine o'clock," Dad said, as we piled out of the car.

"Okay, Dad."

"Thanks, Mr. Tubb," said Louise as she slipped out of the back seat.

"Yeah, thanks, Mr. Tubb," echoed Lisa, Brenda and Carla as each hopped out of the car.

"I wanna do the combhumming boat," demanded my sweet unspoiled little sister.

I was just about to tell her that if she did it would have to be over the dead body of her older sister when Dad intervened, "No, no, Bitsey. Daddy has a surprise for you waiting back home."

"What's the surprise?"

"Well, if I tell you it won't be a surprise, will it?"

"Good ol Dad," I thought as the car pulled away. The five of us were left standing outside of Barkley's Barn.

"Hi, everybody," called Melissa, waving at us from just inside the barn door. We all hurried over to her.

"Are we the first ones here?" Brenda asked, looking around.

"Gosh, no," Melissa said. "There are lots of high school kids working on the float. I was waiting for all of you. I didn't want to be the only one from junior high. Come on, let's go in."

As we followed her into the barn, I seemed to be having a little trouble breathing. I didn't know about the other girls, but I was almost dying of excitement. Just imagine . . . seventh-graders being allowed to work on the float of the high school cheerleaders! Mrs. Volumous had almost been trampled to death in our rush to get permission slips when she asked us if we would consider helping with the float.

We stood for a moment gazing at the half-finished float.

"Oh, gosh," breathed Brenda.

"Look how big it is . . . why it's enormous!" commented Lisa. "Divine!"

I was too awestruck to say anything. All I could do was to stand there with my mouth open. What appeared before us was a giant stork carrying a huge baby. Under the stork was a sign with the words, "DELIVER US A VICTORY."

"Well, hello there. What a nice surprise to see you two here."

Hearing that voice again made a shiver run up and down my spine. It was Nick . . . Mr. Beautiful . . . the lifeguard at Lake Kickapoo. We turned slowly to look at him as he walked toward us and, as usual, were completely dazzled by his smile.

"Hi, Nick, how are you?" Louise greeted him.

All I could manage to croak out was, "Oh . . . Nick."

I knew my face had turned a bright pink.

"Do you know *him*?" Lisa whispered.

Louise whispered back, "We met him at the lake last summer. He was a lifeguard. Isn't he something."

"Dreamy," Brenda said quietly.

"Divine. Really *divine*!"

I thought I was going to have to be revived by the rescue squad. He was even more handsome than I remembered.

"It's sure nice to see both of you," Nick went on.

"Y-y-yes," I stuttered, probably making a wonderful impression on him.

Louise, composed as usual, replied, "Nice to see you too, Nick. Isn't this exciting!"

"Well, we can't just stand here, girls, there's work to be done. This old bird will have to be stuffed if she's ever going to fly in time for homecoming," said Nick as one of the high school cheerleaders walked over to us."

"I'll take over here, Nick," she said. "Now, girls, if you can tear yourselves away, I'll show you what has to be done."

Taking a last long look at Nick, we turned and followed her over to the back of the float.

"Here. All you have to do is this. Watch how I do it," ordered our instructor.

She proceeded to twist a tissue and stuff it into the chicken wire that was attached to the base of the float.

"See?"

We all nodded, we did indeed see.

"Good. You girls can finish the base." Nick had been watching with us. "Julie and I will begin helping the others stuff the bird."

The five of us began working immediately, doing just what Julie had demonstrated. Take a tissue, twist, and stuff. Take a tissue, twist, and stuff. It was monotonous work, but I was anything but bored.

I thought, "This must be what it feels like to be an adult," and reveled in my own maturity.

"Gosh, do you think the float will be done in time?" Melissa asked.

"Well, there are still three more days to work on it," said Louise.

"Anyway, there are lots more high school kids coming later," Lisa said.

I had finally regained some sort of composure and was able to ask, "How do you know?"

"My sister Lori told me," she answered. "I heard her making plans with her boyfriend on the phone last night. He's not picking her up until nine o'clock."

Our conversation was interrupted by Nick . . . a heavenly interruption . . . hollering to another high school boy, "Joe, I think we'd better see if the wings work."

"Sure thing, Nick."

"Come on, everybody, tell us how they look," Nick ordered.

We watched in amazement as Nick and Joe opened a small door in the back of the stork's body and climbed inside, pulling the door shut behind them.

"Stand back!" Nick's voice was a little muffled.

Very, very slowly, the cumbersome wings began to glide up and down, up and down. The barn erupted with cheers and applause.

"Wow," said Louise, "this is really a fantastic float!"

"It sure is," I agreed.

"Who do you suppose is going to make the wings flap in the parade?" Lisa asked.

"Well, it can't be Nick. He's the star quarterback," I explained. "Probably some of the other high school guys."

As it turned out, I couldn't have been more wrong. The wing flappers they had in mind were definitely *not* high school boys. The awful truth soon became apparent. The *real* reason the junior high school cheerleaders were so honored as to be invited to ride on the high school float was revealed to us by none other than Nick.

"Okay, girls," he said, stepping out of the stork. He was looking directly at us. I pointed to myself, unable to understand what he meant.

"Yeah, sure, Ernie. You and Louise and your friends. Come on up. We have to see if you can manage these wings."

The five of us stood there — dumbfounded. How could this be happening to us? How could it be happening to me — Ernestine Cecelia Tubb, who had had great visions of herself riding on the float, graciously waving to the assembled throng? None of us moved. It was as if we had suddenly been cast in bronze.

I was sure the others were having the very same thoughts that I was . . . what a wonderful way to ride in the homecoming parade . . . inside Big Bird's stomach! What a let down.

Not wanting Nick to know just how disappointed I really was, I broke out of the bronze cast and stepped forward. The others followed my lead.

As we stood there, peering into the very small inner space of the stork, Nick said, "Who wants to try it first?"

Personally, I felt that being dipped in boiling tar would have been better, but, good sport that I am, I volunteered, "I will."

"That's my girl," said Nick.

I nearly passed out . . . right there in front of everyone Nick had said "my girl!" I was in such a daze I don't even remember going through the little doorway. The next thing I knew I was inside, trying to fit onto one of those stupid little stools. I really didn't know how Nick and Joe were able to maneuver. Soon Louise was attempting to straddle the other stool.

Our instructions came from the outside.

"Now, girls, grab the two-by-twos and pull down, very slowly."

Louise and I grimaced at each other but did as we were told. Louise groaned under the terrific strain.

"Good grief, these wings are heavy," I complained.

"Yeah, tell me."

Nick was calling encouraging words from outside, "Oh, you're doing great. Just great. Now, let the handles up so the wings go down. Slowly, very slowly. We don't want the wings to break off."

"No, we have to be careful of the wings," I muttered to Louise. "It doesn't matter if our arms break off though."

"Right, Ernie. Who cares?"

"Okay. Super job. Come on out now and let someone else have a turn."

Gladly. I didn't care if someone else wanted my turn. I would be happy to give it up to her. Louise and I, rubbing our arms, made our descent, and Melissa and Brenda took our places.

You may recall that Melissa is the smallest of all of us. That's why she was the top of our ill-fated pyramid. Now being the smallest does not necessarily mean being the weakest. In her case, however, this was true. I mean to tell you, her wing didn't budge an inch . . . there wasn't even a flutter. We seemed to have a wounded stork, one wing flapping up and down, the other motionless.

"Not so hard in there," cautioned Nick. "You're knocking some of the tissue out of the chicken wire."

"Sorry," called Brenda from inside, lowering her wing in a semi-graceful flap.

It was the same with Lisa and Carla. In their case, it was Carla who couldn't move the wing . . . not even a *divine* fraction of an inch.

I could see the handwriting on the barn wall. Carla and Melissa were to be spared the ignominy of riding in our very first homecoming parade in the interior of a stork, working their arms to the bone. No, it fell to Brenda, Louise, Lisa and yours truly to be interred in the chamber of horrors . . . left to struggle as best we could with those giant wings . . . for the duration of the parade.

"How much worse a nightmare could it be?" I asked myself.

I should never have wondered . . . my question was soon to be answered.

CHAPTER FOURTEEN

It was the night of the homecoming game. The float, I'm sorry to say, had been completed, so there was no way to escape our wing-flapping duties. I kept hoping a tornado would come along and demolish Barkley's barn, but, of course, Ernestine Cecelia Tubb never has that kind of luck. So, there we were, sitting in the stands, watching the football game. At least we were *trying* to watch it but it was very difficult with Murphy and his stupid friends sitting directly in back of us. Then too, Bitsey was not far from me and I'm always aware of hovering disaster created by her crazy mixed-up mouth.

"Hey, hey, hey . . . it must be Halloween. Everyone in front of us is in costume. Really *dumb* costumes!"

Oh, yes . . . we cheerleaders were wearing our cos . . . outfits since we were riding on/in the float. It had been decided that Brenda and Lisa would take their turn in the torture chamber for the first half of the parade, then would switch places with Louise and me. That way we'd get to breathe some fresh air and wave to the stands a little while at least.

"Hey, Murph."

"Whatcha want, Al?"

"I sure hope the cheerleaders do their famous 'V for Victory' cheer tonight."

I glanced at the other girls and made a face, but was able to keep from saying anything. We were doing our best to pretend they weren't there, hopeless as that would be.

"Oh, yeah, Al. Isn't that the one with the collapsing pyramid. It oughta be called the Humpty Dumpty cheer."

At that, the idiots almost fell off their seats laughing so hard over what they perceived as their cleverness.

The shrill scream of "Ernie . . . hi, Ernie," came from the next section of bleachers.

The piercing voice, all too readily recognizable, was one that I simply ignored. But I should have known sweet little Bitsey would persist.

"Hi, Ernie," was repeated in a much louder shrill.

"Hey, Ernie," spouted off someone from behind me, "it's not a bit nice to ignore your little sister. You oughta just be glad she recognized you in your Halloween costume."

"Have you guys ever seen a meaner sister in all you life? Just imagine . . . not saying hi to your darling little sister."

"Wow . . . sure haven't, Murph."

"Someone's sure cruel and heartless."

"HI, ERNIE!"

I saw that I'd have to do something to shut up all of the bigmouths so, giving Louise an exasperated look, hollered, "Hi, Bitsey."

"Hey, hey, hey . . . the masqueraded marvel can really talk, how about that!"

"IS IT TIME, ERNIE?"

I couldn't believe this was happening. At this rate I'd be glad to step inside Big Bird.

"No!" I yelled back.

By now, some of the people in the stands were turning and staring. It was so embarrassing. At least Nick was on the field and not a witness to what was going on.

"Why don't my parents gag her?" I whispered to Louise.

"HOW MUCH LONGER, ERNIE?"

"Oooooo . . . isn't that just adorable, guys? Ernie has a date with her little sister."

A chorus of "Ooooooooooooooooooooo's" sounded from the dopes behind us.

Now I realize a junior high school girl should be able to stay in control at all times, but I also realized this would be just too much for anyone to bear. I jumped up and shouted, "Bitsey . . . I will be there when it is time!"

I sat back down quickly, but the damage was done. Giggling and laughter sounded all around us. I'm sure my face was a bright red. I didn't think it was possible for her to embarrass me more than she had already, but her next shout proved me wrong.

"SANK YOU, ERNIE. ERNIE . . . DO YOU WANT SOME OF MY BOPPED CORN?"

An absolute roar of laughter went up. I just sat there looking at my feet.

"Hey, guys . . . how many of you want some of the bopped corn? I bet good old Ernie would share?"

"Is it anything like POPCORN?"

"Sure, Al . . . only instead of it being popped it's bopped."

For the next few minutes of the game all we heard were requests for bopped corn. There were no further communications from little miss loud-speaker. Evidently Mom or Dad finally got control of her. I was relieved to see that only a few minutes remained in the first half.

"We'd better be going," Brenda said.

"Thank goodness," I replied, already on my feet.

Louise reminded me, "We have to pick up Bitsey."

"Don't worry," I told her. "Just try getting out of these stands without her. Believe me, she hasn't taken her eyes off us for one second."

We started moving out of our row and, right on cue, came the call of "WAIT, ERNIE, WAIT. I BE THERE!"

At this remark, the entire area surrounding us erupted in laughter.

"Can you believe her?" I really didn't expect an answer but Louise, as always, defended her, "Oh, Ernie, she's so funny."

"Funny . . . hah!"

Cries of "Wait, Ernie, wait. I be there," came from the idiot row.

My parents and the holy terror must have been sitting on the aisle because Bitsey and Dad were waiting for us when we reached the bottom of the stands. Dad gave me an I'm sorry look and handed Bitsey over to us. Louise took her hand and off we went in the direction of the floats.

Big Bird seemed to loom over us in a menacing way as we approached. I should have taken this for an omen and kept going until I reached the car. The evening would have ended much better if I had locked myself in it right then and there.

The high school cheerleaders were still cheering for the team, so we had a little while to wait.

"Boy, it sure looks different out of the barn," Lisa commented.

"Doesn't it though," Melissa agreed.

"It really does have a kind of eerie look, doesn't it?" said Louise.

"Do you think we should get in yet?" asked Lisa.

"Good grief!" I answered. "Personally I would wait until the very last minute. No, make that the very last second."

We all jumped as the gun went off signaling the end of the first half.

"Now remember," Louise told Lisa, "you and Brenda will have to get out of there fast. Ernie and I will need time to squeeze in before the parade makes it around the track to the visitor's side."

"Well, you'll have to let us know when to come out."

"Whenever it is, it won't be too soon to suit me," I said.

Just then, the high school cheerleaders came running up and climbed to their places on the float. Nick's friend, Julie, called out, "Everybody ready?"

"Just about," Louise called, helping Brenda and Lisa squeeze into place.

"Boy . . . you can't see a thing in here," Lisa complained from the depths of Big Bird. "At least there was some light in the barn."

I tried to comfort her by saying, "There should be some light when we get to the track."

I felt a tugging on my skirt and heard a rather subdued voice asking, "Where me go?"

In all of the excitement, I had completely forgotten about Bitsey . . . I must have wanted to deny that she was there. I guess she must have been so overwhelmed by the float that she hadn't opened her mouth until then.

"Over here, Bitsey. Come and sit next to me," called Louise.

The two of them settled down at the rear of the float. I did the same after closing the stork's back door. We had only just positioned ourselves when the public address system announced the start of the parade. The high school band began to play and our float rolled slowly toward the track. I have to admit I was more than just a little thrilled about being there. Just then I didn't even care that the reason was because the high school cheerleaders wanted their big dumb bird to fly.

As the float came within view of the stands, I hollered to our undercover workers, "You can start flapping now!"

Louise told Bitsey, "Don't forget to wave and smile at all the people."

"I won't, Wheeze."

"Tweet, tweet. Hi, Bitsey. Whatcha doing up there?"

"Hi, Chester. Look at me."

"Chester, what are you doing here?" I asked indignantly.

"Tweet, tweet. My mommy said I could get closer so I could see the parade."

"Well, I'm certain she didn't mean you should get this close. Now get back."

I had an idea that his mother wanted to enjoy the parade without the company of little tweetie bird.

"Tweet, tweet. I don't have to. Tweet, tweet. Mommy said I could come out here."

I looked at Louise and sighed, "Wouldn't you know it! Wouldn't you just know it!"

"Chester, you can ride up here with me," called the magnanimous little mascot.

"Oh, no he can't!"

"Tweet, tweet. I don't want to ride."

Louise laughed, "Well, he fits in with the theme of our float. At least, he's a bird."

By now we were passing directly in front of the stands. We all were waving at the crowd that clapped as our float went by. Brenda and Lisa were doing a super job. The wings were gliding up and down smoothly. Nobody seemed to take any notice of Chester-the-talking-bird walking alongside us. I marveled at how well everything was going. I should have waited for, as we got to the section of the stand where my parents were, little miss public adress system literally screamed at the top . . . and I do mean the very top . . . of her lungs, "HI, MOMMY! HI, DADDY! LOOK AT ME!"

Of course, this brought down the house. People were almost hysterical . . . except for those on the float. Rest assured that Ernestine Cecelia Tubb saw nothing to laugh at. Apparently, neither did the high school cheerleaders who all turned and glared at her.

Thank goodness our float finally reached the end zone so we were no longer a public spectacle. The only drawback was that it was time for Louise and me to enter the big bird.

We jumped up and I hollered, "Okay, Lisa . . . Brenda."

As soon as I opened the door the two galley slaves, eager to be freed, dislodged themselves. Not however, without a lot of moaning and groaning.

"Oh, my poor arms," said Brenda, as Louise and I squeezed past her.

"Good luck," she added.

Lisa, closing the door after us, echoed, "Yeah . . . good luck!"

I heard Brenda say, "You can sit here with me, Bitsey."

"Sank you, Bendy."

In the darkness of Big Bird's stomach Louise's disembodied voice floated toward me, "I hope nothing goes wrong."

"Oh, Louise . . . don't be silly. What could possibly go wrong?"

I would find out what could possibly go wrong . . . all that could possibly go wrong . . . within a few minutes!

CHAPTER FIFTEEN

Peering in what I thought was Louise's direction I said, "I guess it takes a while for your eyes to adjust to the darkness. I can almost see you."

"It's okay, Ernie. We must be getting close to the field lights again. They'll help us see better."

"Not that there's much to see inside a big bird's stomach."

"Boy, Ernie, you can sure say that again!"

"Not that there's much . . ."

"Oh, Ernie, don't get me laughing. This old bird might *really* fly!"

Brenda hollered, "Begin flapping!"

"Make birdie go flip-flappy!" ordered the mascot.

"Right. Now . . . together . . . one, two, three, begin."

Louise groaned as she pulled down on her wing.

"Good grief," I moaned, "it's harder than I remembered."

"I know what you mean," Louise gasped. "And it's so hot and stuffy in here."

"It sure is. We're going to look like two dishrags when — if — we get out of here."

Up and down . . . nice and slow . . . one smooth movement from the two of us. One, two, three . . . easy does it. That's what Nick had told us. Up and down . . . nice and slow . . . One, two, three . . . easy does it. Well, I had news for him. Easy doesn't do it.

A voice fluttered through the outside, "Tweet, tweet. Good wings, Ernie."

I would have taken this as a compliment from anyone else. But I found it rather difficult to be flattered by a third-grade ding-bat who thinks he's a bird. I tried to ignore him by remaining silent. Besides, I needed all my breath to make those enormously heavy wings move.

Chester, however, seems to have learned persistence — if nothing else — from Bitsey.

"TWEET, TWEET. I SAID GOOD WINGS, ERNIE!"

"Good grief, Chester, I can't talk now."

Lisa said, "Little boy, why don't you go sit down and just *watch* the parade."

"Tweet, tweet, I don't have to. My mommy said I don't have to."

"Chester, see me wave at all the peoples," commanded Bitsey.

"Tweet, tweet. I can wave too."

"How cute that must be," I said to Louise, in a voice loaded with sarcasm.

"I can wave to more peoples than you can. I'm riding on the combhumming boat."

"Tweet, tweet. I can wave to more. I'm walking."

"Great Scott, Louise, can't you just see those two having a waving contest out there? Almost makes you glad to be in here

... *almost.*"

I had no sooner said these words than the forerunner of the colossal tragedy began to take shape. My hands were damp because of the excessive heat and, as I pulled hard on the two-by-two, they slipped. Big bird's right wing came crashing down with a thud!

"What happened?" Louise gasped.

"The darn handle slipped out of my hands."

"Are you alright in there?" Brenda hollered.

I didn't take time to answer. I felt around in the dark for the stupid handle.

Brenda hollered again, "Are you okay?"

"Get that wing moving," added Julie.

Just then, I found the handle.

"Okay, okay," I yelled.

"Make birdie go flip-flappy again!"

"Tweet, tweet. Wings not so good, Ernie."

I really didn't need any criticism from our little feathered friend ... feather-brained, that is.

I pulled hard on the handle ... nothing happened. I pulled again ... still nothing. It was stuck on something.

"Will you *please* get that wing going *now*!" hollered another high school cheerleader.

"I'm trying ... I'm trying," I groaned.

Louise hollered, "It's stuck on something out there."

I heard her wing bump to a standstill on the float as she moved over to help me. We both tugged on the handle, but it wouldn't budge. One of the other big-shot high school cheerleaders shouted, "Get a move on in there!"

Louise yelled back. "We're trying!"

Then I heard Melissa say, "Look ... it's caught on the chicken wire!"

"Well ... uncatch it!" hollered another big-shot.

"Here goes," Melissa hollered.

Little did she, or anyone else, know just what she was saying when she uttered the phrase, "Here goes." A chain reaction — like no other one you have ever seen or likely imagined — set in when Melissa unhooked the wing tip from the chicken wire. If you will ... recall that Louise and I were pulling down on the wing's handle with all of our combined strength. I mean to tell you, we were practically hanging from that stupid thing. Therefore, when Melissa released the stuck wing, not only did the wing flap up ... it shot up ... with such a force that it simply kept on going right over Big Bird's body.

Now, since the wing was connected to the body, the momentum took the whole entire thing right with it. That wing and body did a somersault to end all somersaults right in front of everybody in the stands ... the entire stadium crowd. It then quietly came to rest next to the float.

An unbelieving crowd hushed as everyone stared. Louise and I really didn't know what to do. We just sat down on our stools again. The other riders on the float looked as if they had been mortally wounded. In the next instant, the crowd went wild.

I was unable to do anything except sit there on the little stool in the center of what had once been a great homecoming float. I thought, "My, my Ernestine ... only two and a half months into your junior high school career and what have you done? Managed to embarrass yourself at least one hundred times and now . . . now, you have wrought a disaster so great that it will never be forgotten. You have ruined the entire homecoming parade."

The only possible comforting thought was the knowledge that the worst certainly had to be over. Nothing else of this magnitude could possibly happen.

Hah! What a laugh!

I should have realized as I sat there on the stool . . . a forlorn, pathetic figure . . . in front of a stadium gone wild with laughter, that it was only the beginning.

Ernestine Cecelia Tubb was yet to have the most amazing adventures ever chronicled in the history of the Cecil T. Squat Junior High School.